Knocked off course

"This is big, Nancy, really big. The guy that told me is in the know and everything."

I wanted to reach down into his throat with both hands and pull the words out. But I forced myself to stay calm. Sometimes getting Charlie to tell me something is like trying to get a cat out from under the bed for a trip to the vet.

"It's okay," I said in a low voice. "What happened?"

I held my breath so long waiting for Charlie's answer, I could feel a warm flush in my cheeks.

"It's the money," Charlie finally said. "The Biking for Bucks pledges." He shook his head, and his eyes widened into almost perfect circles.

"What about the money?" I prompted, although I had a feeling that I knew what he was going to say.

"It's gone," he said. "It's all gone."

NANCY DREW
girl detective™

Available from Aladdin Paperbacks

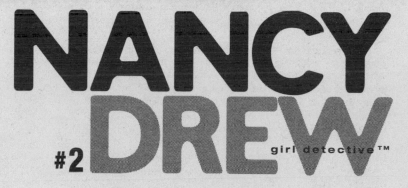

NANCY DREW

#2 **girl detective™**

A Race Against Time

CAROLYN KEENE

Aladdin Paperbacks

New York   London   Toronto   Sydney

First Aladdin Paperbacks edition March 2004

Copyright © 2004 by Simon & Schuster, Inc.

ALADDIN PAPERBACKS
An imprint of Simon & Schuster Children's Publishing Division
1230 Avenue of the Americas, New York, NY 10020

Manufactured in the United States of America

30

NANCY DREW and colophon are registered trademarks of
Simon & Schuster, Inc.

NANCY DREW: GIRL DETECTIVE is a trademark of
Simon & Schuster, Inc.

Library of Congress Control Number 2003109055

ISBN-13: 978-0-689-86567-1
ISBN-10: 0-689-86567-8

0809 Offset Paperback Manufacturers Inc. Dallas, PA

Contents

Ditched in the Creek

My name is Nancy Drew, and I've always had this rule: If you're in the game, you play to win.

That doesn't mean I'm cutthroat competitive. But it *does* mean that if I make a commitment, I'll see it through to the end.

Unfortunately it's not always easy. I've discovered that sometimes one rule is canceled out by another. And that's exactly what happened last weekend during the River Heights Biking for Bucks charity road race.

I'm an amateur detective, so another one of my rules is: Solve the crime. And even though I was the sprinter of my cycling team, and it was my job to bring us over the finish line in first place—

Okay, I'm getting a little ahead of myself. I do that

when I get excited. I'm going to back up and start where the problems did—at the beginning.

I live in River Heights. It's a small Midwestern town on the Muskoka River. At first it looks like one of those sleepy burgs where everyone lies around on porch swings in the summertime, drinking lemonade and patting dogs. But it's really a cool town, packed with lots of interesting people.

Every year Biking for Bucks raises a lot of money for the Open Your Heart Fund, which helps residents who are having trouble making ends meet. Everyone in town gets involved in some way, and it's become a major two-day festival.

This year my team is made up of my two best friends—Bess Marvin and George Fayne—and my boyfriend, Ned Nickerson.

The evening before the race, my team joined the other five teams at the CarboCram in the convention center downtown.

I wore my good-luck sweater. It was *originally* sky blue, one of my favorite colors. Bess helped me pick it out years ago. She said it matched my eyes and looked good with my hair, which is that unusual color some people call strawberry blond. I don't give much thought to things like this, but Bess does. I like that sweater because it's like a favorite pair of jeans—the more you wear it, the softer it gets. Style's okay, of course, but give me comfort every time.

Anyway, through the years I've worn that sweater before several competitions I've been in, and it's always seemed to bring me good luck. So in the name of tradition—or superstition—I wore it that evening to the CarboCram. Even though it was a little worn out and faded.

We didn't come just for the pasta, vegetables, and fruit. We were also getting the info pack, turning in our pledges and money, and checking out the competition.

All the teams had asked friends, family, neighbors, and even strangers to pledge money to support their efforts in the race. Supporters pledged to donate money for every mile the team completed and to give extra money if the team came in first, second, or third.

I arrived with Bess and George and we were sitting at a long table, eating spaghetti. Ned was late.

"I collected hundreds of dollars more this year than I did last year," Bess told us, showing George and me the contents of her envelope.

It's pretty easy for Bess to gather pledges. She has wavy blond hair, big blue eyes with superlong lashes, perfect teeth, and a perfect nose. She's one of those

natural beauties who make some people jealous—
except she's so nice and so *real* that nearly everyone
ends up crazy about her. And those who aren't just
don't know her well enough yet.

"From what I've heard," George said, "everyone's
been pretty generous this year. Biking for Bucks
should set a new record for fund-raising."

George's name is really Georgia, but she likes her
nickname much better. She and Bess are cousins, but
you'd never guess by looking at them. They have
hardly anything in common—except me, of course.
George has dark brown hair and eyes and is a lot
taller and leaner than Bess. George is the athlete, Bess
is the fan. That's why George would be our lead-out
rider in the race, and Bess would be driving the support truck.

"Where's Ned?" Bess asked, checking her watch.
"Still hanging out at school, right?"

"He had a special seminar at the university," I told
her, "but he said he'd be here by now. He'll show up
eventually. He wouldn't turn down free pasta."

"Are you sure?" George said. "It sounds crazy, but
sometimes I think he'd rather read than eat! It seems
like once he gets lost in a book, he's off in another
world."

George was right, and I was actually a little annoyed

with Ned. I reminded him twice to be sure and get back from the university in time for the CarboCram. I thought it was important that all the members of our team get together the night before the race and go over our strategy one last time.

"Did I tell you my whole family is coming for the race start tomorrow morning?" Bess asked. "What about your dad? Will he be home in time?"

"Not for the start," I answered. "He won't get back to town until tomorrow night. He'll be there for the finish, of course."

My dad is Carson Drew, the best attorney in River Heights—no question. My mom died when I was three years old, and that's been hard to deal with sometimes. But Dad has always been there for me, and I can totally count on him. He'd been at the state capital for the week before the race, working on a big case. But he said he'd be back to see me roll across the finish line, so I knew he'd be there.

"Is the truck packed?" George asked Bess as she wound a big bite of pasta around her fork.

"Totally," Bess answered, sipping her juice. "I've got complete camping equipment for all of us—food, bike maintenance and repair stuff, everything we'll need. George, I even packed your spare bike and a couple of extra pairs of biking shorts and jerseys in our colors. It won't hurt to have backups on hand, just in case."

"I'm so hyped about the GPS," George said, as she read the race fact sheet. "I love that tracking system. And it says here the race organizers lock them on so they can't be removed or switched around until the end of the race. And they can't be altered. A friend showed one to me—even *I* can't break into this thing—so far, anyway."

George is our resident electronic genius. She's not only a computer geek and an ace at getting me information through the Internet, she's also an expert at rigging electronic equipment into the most incredibly handy tools.

"The GPS is to make sure each team follows the rules, right?" Bess asked.

"Absolutely," I replied. "Each team has to ride the same course. And everyone has to stop, eat, and camp overnight at the same time. The GPS guarantees that no one cheats."

"Speaking of cheats," George muttered, "prime example at ten o'clock."

"Well, look who's here—the famous Nancy Drew!"

I didn't need to glance up to know who was talking. I've heard that same whiny voice since the first grade.

"Deirdre," I said, finally looking up. "I saw your name on the list. Who's on your team?"

"Evan and Thad Jensen," Deirdre answered. "Malcolm Price is driving our truck." I recognized the names, but didn't really know any of them. It was typical of her to surround herself with a team of guys.

"Looks like your team is short one rider," she added. She glanced around at Bess, George, and me without making any real eye contact. "Where's Ned?" she continued. "Shouldn't he be here with the rest of you? Don't tell me he stood you up! Doesn't he have class this afternoon? Maybe he got stuck at the university."

Deirdre is one of those girls who's really hard to like because she seems to go out of her way to be as obnoxious as possible. She's very striking in a Cruella kind of way—black hair, green eyes, really pale skin. But she's self-centered to the extreme. She seems to think the world revolves around her—or at least that it *should*.

I ignored her crack about Ned. She's always had her eye on him, and everyone knows it. But frankly, I don't see her as any real competition in that department. It's like my dad says: "The Drews can always take the Shannons."

Deirdre's father is also a big-time attorney, but when he and my dad meet as opponents in court, my dad usually wins. I intend to continue that family reputation.

"Ned's fine," I told Deirdre. "But it was kind of you to ask." I flashed her my sweetest smile. I've learned that the best way to deal with her is to keep her off balance. And the best way to do that is to not do what she expects me to do. Smiling is the *perfect* response when she's trying to get to me.

"Dad bought me the greatest new bike for the race," Deirdre said. I always know I've won a round with her if she changes the subject abruptly.

"Really?" I said, still smiling.

"It's got everything," she rattled on. "It's Italian—made of the same alloy they use in fighter jets. Custom-made frame, forty-five gears, unified pedal/shoe cleats, gel saddle, aero bars, titanium spokes. Five thousand dollars plus."

"Sounds great, DeeDee," George said, standing up. "See you at the finish line—we'll be waiting there for you." She left the table and headed back to the food line.

Deirdre's white cheeks flushed little spots of pink for a minute or two when George used her grade-school nickname.

"Yeah? Well, we'll see who gets there first, *Georgia.*" Deirdre's comeback was pretty lame, but I knew she'd gotten to George, since George hated to be called by her full name.

"You're surely not riding a bike, Bess," Deirdre said, turning her forked tongue on a new prey. "You must be the truck—"

Bweep . . . Bwirrrr. The irritating sound of microphone feedback interrupted the irritating sound of Deirdre's voice.

"Ladies and gentlemen . . . ladies and gentlemen . . . if you'll take your seats, please."

One of the race organizers, Ralph Holman, spoke from the large stage in the corner of the room. Deirdre sidled away and rejoined her team at a table up front.

"It's great to see you all," Mr. Holman said. "We have scheduled the weather to be perfect tomorrow and Sunday, so let's have a great time and break a few records. As you know, this race is sponsored by the Mahoney Foundation and benefits the Open Your Heart Fund, and its grand trophy is donated by Mrs. Cornelius Mahoney."

A large cheer rang out and most of us stood up to show our respect for Mrs. Mahoney. Her husband was the only descendant of Ethan Mahoney, an original settler here in the nineteenth century. When Ethan recognized that he was sitting on top of a huge lode of iron ore, he founded Mahoney Anvil Corporation. That was a stroke of genius. Now, a century later, Mrs. Mahoney controls the Mahoney Foundation, which is worth billions of dollars.

We stopped clapping and cheering and sat down again, just as George returned with another plate piled high with food. "Ned isn't here yet?" she whispered, looking around the room. "Do you suppose you should try to check in with him?"

She'd read my mind. I already had my hand on my cell phone and was pushing his speed-dial number. I wasn't annoyed anymore—I was concerned. Ned can sometimes get distracted, but he would *never* intentionally miss anything this important. Not without letting me know.

His phone rang a long time before I was transferred to his voice mail. "Hey, Ned," I spoke softly into the phone, "we're all cramming carbs and we miss you. Give me a call on my cell phone, okay?"

I switched the phone from ring to vibrate, and held it tightly as Mrs. Mahoney took the microphone.

"Hello, everyone," she said. Her voice sounded reedy, but proud. Her hair is always smooth and shiny, and even when she's dressed simply in a blazer and slacks, like she was that evening, she always looks like she stepped out of a fashion magazine.

"Thank you for participating in this weekend's exciting race," Mrs. Mahoney continued. "Your dedication to this wonderful cause warms my heart, and certainly would have pleased my dear husband very much."

Mrs. Mahoney was a little blinded by love when she referred to Cornelius Mahoney as "dear." According to everyone who knew him—including my father—he was anything but dear. Most remember her husband as a pretty nasty guy, and he was probably a crook and securities manipulator. Mrs. Mahoney always refers to him as a generous man, however. And, since people like her a lot more than they disliked Cornelius, no one questions her memories.

I was listening to her, but just barely. My real concentration was on the cell phone in my hand. I couldn't shake this uneasy feeling I was getting about Ned.

"Remember," Mrs. Mahoney said, "you're not only competing for this." With a grand gesture she swept her arm toward the pedestal beside her. Balanced securely on top was a large statue of an anvil that had been painted gold. "Winning the anvil is a great honor, of course," Mrs. Mahoney continued, "but the real privilege is being able to do something for those less fortunate than we are. Thank you especially for joining the race to help others."

During the second round of cheers I felt my phone vibrate. My heart seemed to stop for a moment and then it began racing. I gestured to Bess and George that I was leaving the table, and went into the hall so I could hear.

"Hi," I answered the phone, my heart still pounding. "I'm so glad you finally called."

"Hi, Nancy. It's James Nickerson." The low voice of Ned's father rumbled through the receiver.

I was sure it was going to be his son. My mind raced with questions about Ned and his whereabouts. I was so preoccupied with my own thoughts, actually, that it took me a minute to bring my attention back to the voice in my ear.

"I'm sorry, Mr. Nickerson," I said. "What did you say?"

"I said I know you're at an event, so I won't keep you," Mr. Nickerson repeated. "Can I speak to Ned? His phone isn't on."

"Ned isn't here," I told him. "In fact, I just left him a message myself a few minutes ago. He must still be at the university."

"No, he's not. That's why I'm calling you there."

I could hear the irritation in Mr. Nickerson's voice. "I just talked to Professor Herman. He said Ned left at the end of class a couple of hours ago. Look, just have him give me a call when he gets there, okay?"

"Sure," I answered. I flipped my phone shut and walked back into the CarboCram.

Bess met me halfway to the table. "Charlie Adams is here," she said. "He wants to talk to you. How's Ned? Where is he? When is he getting over here?"

"I don't have a clue," I answered. I quickly told her about my phone conversation with Mr. Nickerson. I finished just as George and Charlie walked up.

Charlie is a sort of local hero of mine. He drives the emergency truck for the best auto garage in town. So usually when I see him it's to thank him for pulling me out of a ditch, or for bringing a tire to replace both the blowout I just had *and* the flat spare tire in the trunk, or for jump-starting a dead battery. But not this time.

"Charlie, hi," I greeted him. "What can I do for you?"

"Hi, Nancy," he said. "You look great. I sure hope your team wins the race."

"Thanks, Charlie. Is there something wrong with my car I don't know about?"

"Nope," he answered. "And not with Ned's anymore either. I fixed it all up and it's waiting for him to pick up."

"What do you mean?" I asked.

"What was wrong with Ned's car?" Bess followed up.

"Nothing a little tow and a few hammer blows couldn't fix. He went only partway into that shallow creek. But he banged the front corner into a big boulder. The dent popped right back out when I smacked it, though."

"What creek? What boulder? Start at the beginning, Charlie," I demanded. Sometimes talking to Charlie drives me crazy. He talks in unintentional riddles, and I always feel like I'm walking backward through our conversations.

"Oh, you don't know anything about it, do you?" Charlie finally realized. "Okay. Well, I go on a call. And driving back to town, I look over and see the back end of Ned's car sticking up out of a foot of water in this creek."

"Where?" I asked.

"You know that big sycamore out on Shady Road?" Charlie asked. "It was right there before the curve. But it was no big deal. I pulled Ned's car right out and dragged it back to the garage and fixed it up for him."

14

"But where's Ned now?" I insisted.

"Gee, I don't know about *him*," Charlie answered. "I only found the car. It was empty when I found it. Abandoned."

2

Where's Ned?

"**A**bandoned!" I repeated. "Ned wasn't with his car?"

"He wouldn't just leave it," George pointed out.

"He might have," Bess offered. "You said his phone wasn't on. Okay, so what if it was out of juice, and he couldn't phone for help? He started walking back to town, and . . . then . . . But he'd be here by now, wouldn't he, Nancy? So where is he?"

Bess had asked the question that kept roaring through my mind. *Ned, where are you?*

"Charlie, what time did you find the car?" I asked.

"A few hours ago, I guess. I'd gone out on the other call, but I didn't have to bring that car in. I fixed it while I was there. House-call Charlie, that's my name."

"That's great service," I said with a reassuring smile. "Now, did you see anything around the car that might indicate where Ned went?" I continued. "Any footprints? Something he might have dropped?"

"To tell you the truth, I wasn't looking for anything like that, Nancy," Charlie said. "I figured—like Bess said—Ned's walked on into town, so I'll just take in his car and meet him there. But so far, I haven't seen him."

"Did you check under the hood?" I asked. "Was there anything obvious that might have made him veer off the road? Something with the brakes maybe? Or the steering?"

"I gave it a good once-over," Charlie answered. "Nothing wrong with the brakes or steering. The shocks were good. No tires blown out. You know . . . there weren't even any skid marks on the road. Nothing to show that he'd lost control of the car. When you get right down to it, it didn't look like anything *made* him end up off the road. It's like he just turned the wheel and drove his car into the creek on purpose."

"Okay, thanks, Charlie," I said. I tried to give him a grateful smile, but it didn't come very easily. Finally I gave up and turned away, so I could think in peace.

It's pretty hard to stay calm when someone is telling me that it looks like my boyfriend has driven head-first into a creek.

"I'm going over to the garage," I told Bess and George. "I want to take a look at Ned's car. You two stay here and make sure we get all the race information. I'll come back when I'm finished."

I asked Charlie if he would let me into the garage and followed his road-emergency truck there in my car. He had done his usual perfect work, and Ned's car looked even better than the last time I'd seen it. It sure didn't look as if it had been in an accident that day.

First I checked the wheels to see whether there was anything suspicious stuck in the tire treads. I found nothing but pebbles and a few twigs—the kind of stuff you can't help but pick up when you're just driving around. While Charlie answered the phone in the office, I poked around in the trunk, then climbed inside Ned's car.

A couple of things surprised me. First I found Ned's phone in the glove compartment. It's not like him to forget his phone. He usually throws it in a cargo pocket or wears it on his belt. I dropped it in my backpack, then got in the backseat.

The second surprise was what was going on under

Ned's car seat. He could have had a small yard sale with all that junk!

With an umbrella I found on the backseat, I swept across that dark space under the driver's seat of Ned's car. Sure enough, all sorts of weird stuff rolled out—business cards and birthday cards, a CD, lots of coins and leaves, a couple of pens, a small brass medallion, a computer-printed map, a wrench, and a broken plastic hanger. And that was just from one sweep of the umbrella.

I placed everything on the seat for closer examination. All the paper stuff seemed to make sense, as did the coins, pens, and wrench. I recognized the CD—I had given it to him for his birthday.

In fact, the only thing that looked out of place to me was the brass medallion. I had never seen it before. I wrapped it in a tissue and put it in my pocket. Finding nothing more worth noting under the passenger seat, I waved to Charlie and drove back to the convention center.

In the parking lot I got out Ned's phone and listened to his voice-mail messages—all in the name of detecting, of course. There were only three messages: two from Ned's father, and mine.

When I got back into the convention center, Bess and George were waiting for me in the lobby.

"Perfect timing!" Bess exclaimed. "We just got out."

"Ned still hasn't shown up here," George added. "Did you find out anything when you checked his car?"

"Maybe. But wait here a minute. I want to see if he left any messages with the CarboCram people."

I found one of the women in charge. She checked with several people, but Ned had not called in or left a message with anyone. So I rejoined my friends.

"Nothing," I told them. "He hasn't called in here."

"So tell us what you found in his car," George said.

"His phone, for one thing," I told them. "That's really strange. And it's working."

"So my theory about it being out of power is wrong," Bess said. "But why would he leave it in his car?"

"He wouldn't," I answered. "I also found this." I took out the brass medallion and showed it to them. It was oval shaped with a hole punched on one end. Etched into the metal were two figures that looked like fishing hooks, one hook to the left, one to the right.

"It looks like some kind of symbol," George said.

"Astrology," Bess proclaimed.

"That's it, Bess!" I agreed. "It's Gemini—the twins."

"It could be jewelry," Bess offered. "You could put

a ribbon or cord through that hole and wear it as a necklace."

"Or it could be part of a key chain," George suggested.

"Twins," I repeated. Something was nagging at the back of my mind, but I just couldn't pull it out. I suddenly felt really restless, like I had to move, take some kind of action.

"I'm going to find Ned," I told them, heading out of the lobby. "Let's go out to where Charlie picked up his car."

My friends didn't say anything. They didn't need to. We all just hurried out to the parking lot and piled into my car.

We were really quiet on the way out to Shady Road. After eight more miles I stopped the car under the big old sycamore by the curve.

That tree is famous. Whenever someone writes about the state's largest trees or the most beautiful ones, that white-and-gray sycamore is always a contender. It's not only huge in the trunk, it has these major branches with three-foot diameters that grow straight out before they begin to slope upward. Three or four men could stand side by side on one of those branches and it wouldn't even tremble.

"There it is," George said, racing from the car.

"There's the sycamore. That's where Ned went off the road."

My pulse pounded inside my temples. *Whawmm, whawmm, whawmm, whawmm.* I grabbed my backpack and hurried after George. Bess pounded along behind me.

Ugly tire-tread marks tracked across the road, slashed through the grass and weeds, and stopped in a clump of cattails at the edge of the shallow creek. One set of tracks was much larger than the other and showed double tires. I figured those were probably the marks of Charlie's road-emergency truck.

"Do you think there are any snakes out here?" Bess asked, looking at the weeds. I could barely hear her, her voice was so low.

"If there are, they'll hear us coming and slither away," George said before I could answer.

She sounded impatient with her cousin. That's sometimes the case. They're really close, but sometimes what starts as a difference of opinion can escalate into a full-blown battle. I'm never thrilled to be caught between them.

I stood where Ned's car had been earlier, where it had smashed down all the wild growth. I looked around at the large area of weeds that had been flattened by his car. It was still just light enough to see footprints in the muddy ground near the little creek. There were a bunch of them, and they left the sole designs of three different pairs of shoes.

I walked along beside the footprints. At first they were indentations in the mud. Then they became deposits of mud in the grass. They all eventually led back up to the road. Only one left muddy paces down the road toward River Heights.

"What are you doing?" Bess asked me.

"I'm checking these footprints," I answered. "They look fresh—like they might have been made earlier today."

"But Charlie didn't mention any footprints," George reminded me.

"He said he wasn't really looking for any," I pointed out. "He was probably concentrating on doing *his* job. Now I'm concentrating on doing *mine*."

I followed one set of prints from the location of the driver's door to the water's edge, and again toward the road. These prints stopped in the mud a few yards from where Ned's car had been.

"These could be Charlie's shoe prints," I told my friends, pointing to that particular set. "Look. Here he checked to make sure Ned wasn't still in the car and maybe looked to see if the keys were in it. Then he walked toward the front of the car, probably to check the depth of the water," I reasoned. I followed alongside the prints. "Then it looks like he walked to the back of Ned's car and hooked up the tow."

"These look like the emergency-truck tire prints," George pointed out.

"Right," I agreed. "And here's where he walked to the truck and got in, so he could pull Ned's car out of the creek.

"What about these others?" Bess asked.

"Well, there are two other sets of prints here," I showed them, "which is about where Ned's driver's door would have been. That gives us three sets—one is Ned's obviously. Another is Charlie's. So who belongs to this third set?"

I felt a small stab of worry. Who else stood on this spot, I wondered. And did they do something to Ned. Where *was* he?

The three of us followed the footprints along. "They lead back up to the road," Bess said. "But then they disappear."

"Whoever made them must have gotten into a car or some other vehicle at this point," I suggested.

"You've got a funny look on your face," George noted. "What are you thinking?"

"I just wonder," I answered. "Ned has not shown up anywhere he was supposed to be since this afternoon, and he hasn't called anyone to say why. That is definitely not like him. His car was ditched out here, along with his phone. Maybe *he* was ditched out here too."

I looked around. The countryside now shimmered in a pale gray twilight.

"Ned!" I shouted. "Ned, are you out here?"

3

Linking the Clues

N ed!" I shouted again.

Nothing. Not a sound.

"Ned? Are you out here?"

My voice sounded hoarse, and I realized I was shaking. I'm not usually unduly afraid—and I'm always happy to rescue people. But it's a little different when a good friend is in trouble. It's harder sometimes to keep from being too emotional and losing your focus.

I took a deep breath and cleared my throat. This time my voice was strong and clear. "Ned!" I called out one last time.

I looked around, but there was no one in sight, no buildings, no hiding places. Ned definitely was not out there.

"Let's go," I said, racing to my car. "We're going back to town."

Again my friends didn't say a word as they piled into the car and I pulled out onto Shady Road. We all gazed through the windows, lost in our own thoughts. I had a feeling they were as worried as I was.

We were still silent as I drove back to River Heights—the only car on the road in either direction. The last bits of twilight sparked out, and the sky turned dark gray. I strained my eyes, scanning the sides of the road and the landscape around us.

When I first saw the glimmer ahead, I blinked twice to make sure. The steady light grew stronger the closer I got, and at last I let out a cheer. "There he is!" I shouted. "That's him! I'm sure of it!"

Ahead I saw the rear reflectors of a bike being guided down the road by Ned. I recognized him from a distance immediately, because he was wearing his red windjacket with the fluorescent silver lightning bolt on the back.

I honked the horn, and he turned. When he saw my car he shot his fist in the air and broke into one of those incredible smiles. I skidded to a stop and jumped out of the car. Bess and George followed closely behind.

"It's always great to see you," Ned told me, dropping his bike carefully to the grass beside the road.

"But this time it's especially great. I've got really bad news. Someone stole my car. I always park it under—"

"Your car isn't stolen," I interrupted. "It's at Charlie's."

"Charlie Adams's? What's it doing there?"

"He towed it out of the water earlier," Bess chimed in.

"Water! Whoa—wait a minute. Start at the beginning."

I told Ned about Charlie finding his car.

"*In* the creek?" he asked. "It was actually in the creek? Man, I'm glad Charlie came along when he did."

"I'm so glad we found out about it," Bess said. "That's what prompted Nancy to go out there in the first place."

"I talked to your dad earlier," I told Ned. "He'd called Professor Herman and found out that you'd left the university hours earlier, so I was really concerned."

Ned wrapped his arms around me in a warm hug, and it felt great.

"Where have you been all this time?" George asked Ned.

"Walking," he answered. He stopped and leaned over, resting his hands on his knees. Then he stretched, arching his spine and throwing his head back. At that point I noticed the large rip in his pants leg. It ran from his knee down to his ankle. When he moved, you could glimpse a nasty scrape that zigzagged down the side of his leg.

"Don't tell me you walked from the university!" Bess said.

"Okay," Ned said, reaching for his bike. "I won't tell you that," he said, loading his bike onto the rack on the top of my car, "but that's exactly what I did."

"What *did* happen?" I urged. I didn't want to push him, but I was really eager to find out how his car ended up in the creek.

"I always use my class to get in an extra cycling workout," he answered, as we all got into the car. Bess and George got in back and Ned rode in the front passenger seat. Bess handed him a water bottle, and he took several big slugs. I pulled out on the road and started the few miles back to River Heights.

"On the way to the university," Ned continued, "I always pull my car onto the grass under the big sycamore tree and park. Then I bike the ten miles plus into class."

"Did you do that this afternoon?" George asked.

"I did," Ned reported. "I double-lock my bike on the rack outside the classroom, and I can see it through the window. When I got out of class I started cycling back to my car. I had gone only part of the way when I wiped out." He reached down to check the scrape on his leg.

"Did you hit a rock or something?" Bess asked.

"Nope. My chain busted out, and I went end over end and skidded on my leg." He twisted around in his seat and flashed Bess a resigned smile. "I could have used your expertise on that chain, Bess," he said. "And some of those extra links you always have handy.

"Anyway," he continued, turning back around to look at me. "The worst part was that I'd left my phone in the glove compartment of my car. I was stuck in an isolated area and couldn't even call for help."

"So you walked," I said.

"Yeah, back to where I thought my car was—safely parked under the tree."

"Only Charlie had already seen it in the creek and towed it in," I pointed out.

"So you kept walking," Bess said. "Wow."

"Until I saw an angel driving her blue hybrid to rescue me." Ned reached over and squeezed my shoulder.

"I bet you'll never leave your phone in the glove compartment again," Bess said.

"Or park on an incline without pulling your emergency brake," George added.

"But I did," Ned said, twisting around again. "That's just it. I *always* use the emergency when I park under that tree." He frowned as he narrowed his eyes. He thought for a moment, then nodded firmly. "I definitely pulled that brake this afternoon."

My mind sifted that information into the pot with the rest of Ned's report. What was the *full* story here, I wondered.

"That's quite a hike," George observed, "especially when you're dragging your bike along with you."

"I took the shortcut across Fern Meadow," he said. "That helped a little."

"That's why we didn't see you on our way out to the sycamore," I realized. Suddenly I remembered something. I reached into my pocket and took out the brass medallion with the Gemini symbol that I'd found under his car seat. "Is this yours?" I asked Ned.

"No," he answered. "Why?"

"I found it in your car," I told him. "I was pretty sure it didn't belong to you. Have you ever seen it before?"

"No," he answered, shaking his head. He squinted his eyes as if he were trying to remember something.

Then he shook his head again. "No—I really don't have a clue," he said. "Maybe it's some sort of medal or something. I have no idea why it was under my seat though."

"You're sure you set the emergency brake," I reminded him. "So maybe this was dropped by someone who opened your car and *un*set the brake. Someone who released the brake so that your car would roll into the creek."

"You're saying that it wasn't an accident?" George asked.

"I'm saying that's possible," I confirmed.

"Deirdre," George said in a very low whisper. Then she spoke up. "What about the race tomorrow?" she asked Ned. "Are you up for it?"

"Absolutely," Ned answered. "A long shower, a big meal, and a good night's sleep, and I'll be ready to ride."

"I'm biking the first leg," George reminded him. "So you'll get even more rest in the truck tomorrow morning."

"Excellent," Ned said. "That's all I'm going to need."

"Are you sure?" I asked. "I don't care as much about the race as I do about you."

"I'm sure," he promised. I could tell by the look in his eyes that he meant it. "I'm fine now, and I'm going to be even better tomorrow."

"How about taking a detour to the hospital emergency room," I suggested, "and have someone take a look at your leg. You've got a really bad scrape."

"Not necessary," Ned said. "Really. I'd do it if I thought I needed to."

"Okay." I handed him his phone. "You'd better call your dad."

While he talked to his dad, I went over Ned's story in my mind. Who would want to put Ned out of commission? And why? Did it have anything to do with the race? Or was it something personal against him?

"I didn't tell my dad what happened," Ned said after he hung up. "We've got unexpected houseguests—a couple of his old colleagues here from Washington. I'll wait until they leave, and then give my folks the full story."

"Maybe by then we'll have figured out exactly what *did* happen," I said.

As I pulled back into River Heights, I asked the hardest question. "Ned, is there anyone who would want to harm you for some reason? Have you made any enemies recently?"

"I can't think of anyone," he answered.

"Okay, then, we'll just go with what we've got and see what we can figure out," I assured him. Now if I could only assure myself, I thought pessimistically, we'd be in business.

I took Ned home first—he was really hungry and needed to get that leg wound cleaned up. And besides, I knew a good hot shower would make him feel a lot better.

When we got to his house, Bess told him to just leave the bike on the rack. "I'll repair the chain tonight," she told us, "and make sure the bike is ready for the race."

"As your team captain, I order you to cram some carbs and get a good night's sleep," I told Ned, giving him a kiss. "Bess will pick you up in the morning."

"Go team," he called back as he walked inside. He looked tired, but I knew he'd be back in form by the next day.

"So, tell us, Nancy," Bess said as I backed out of Ned's driveway. "What do you really think happened? Who did this to Ned? And why?"

"I honestly don't know," I answered. "I believe what Ned told us about not having any current enemies."

"Are you sure he'd tell you if he did?" George asked. "What if it's someone really nasty, and he's not telling you so you won't get involved? What if he's just trying to protect you?"

George had a point. Ned doesn't lie, but he some-times hedges the truth for my sake. This wouldn't be the first time he had put my welfare before the pursuit of a case. But this time I believed him. Some-thing in my gut told me he was being totally straight with me. I shook my head.

"What about Deirdre?" George said. "She's not above doing something like this, just to mess with our heads the night before the race."

"I thought about that when you suggested it," I said. "And I'm not ruling her out . . . yet."

I dropped off George next, then drove to Bess's house. They live a few blocks apart off Vernon Avenue.

Bess and I took Ned's bike down off the rack. To-gether we looked at the broken chain. It was easy to see where the broken links had snapped. It was also easy to see that they had been partly filed through before snapping.

Finally I headed home. Hannah Gruen, our housekeeper, had already turned in for the night. When my mother died, Dad hired Hannah to keep house, cook, and baby-sit. But she does much more than that. She's definitely a valued member of our little family.

I wasted no time getting cleaned up and collapsing

into bed. It had been a long day, and it took me a while to wind down my mind. Two trains of thought whizzed along parallel tracks: What happened to Ned? and Is my team ready for the race?

Without answers to either question, I finally gave up and fell asleep.

4

The Race Is On?

Saturday morning's weather lived up to the local forecasters' expectations: It was sunny but not hot, breezy but not blowy, dry, and gorgeous. I called Ned the minute I woke up, and was relieved to hear him say he felt great and ready to ride.

I showered and dressed in my racing gear. Bess had chosen these bright purple biking shorts and jerseys with green stripes for our matching uniforms. Not all the teams went that far, but with Bess on our team, we couldn't help it.

I packed my sports bag with sunscreen, lip balm, a pocketknife, a miniflashlight, a couple of hairclips, my cell phone, energy bars, insect repellant, and other odds and ends. Something told me to grab the Gemini medallion I'd found in Ned's car, so I dropped it in, too. Then I went downstairs to the kitchen.

Hannah had posted a note on the refrigerator telling me she had already left for downtown. She had volunteered to help cook and serve breakfast for the race organizers. The aroma of her homemade banana bread still floated around the room—and a loaf waited for me on the counter.

Although I wasn't scheduled to ride until three o'clock, I was still feeling jumpy and excited. So I decided to down a peach protein smoothie and a piece of Hannah's melt-in-your-mouth bread.

Bess picked me up in the truck she had outfitted for the two-day event. George and Ned were already aboard.

"Hurry up," Bess called to me. "We don't want to be late for all the prerace stuff."

I jumped into the backseat, and we sped away.

"So are we excited or what?" George asked everyone. "I am *so* ready to start this race! We're going to leave Deirdre and her team coughing in our dust."

"I'm ready," Ned said.

"Me too," I chimed in.

Soon we were driving into the parking lot at the bank downtown. The starting line for the race was at

Main Street and Highland Boulevard, right in front of the bank, on one of the busiest corners in town. All the streets in the area had been roped off for the race. Temporary bleachers had been erected on the sidewalks for supporters and fans, and a small stage constructed near the starting line.

Red and gold banners billowed out from all the streetlights, and the storefront windows of all the downtown businesses and shops had handmade posters cheering on their favorite teams. Members of the high school pep band had staked out a spot in the minipark across from the bank, and the air was full of rousing music.

George, Ned, and I unloaded our bikes in the parking lot and did a few warm-ups. I hate racing in brand-new clothes, so I'd worn my new gear for a couple of ten-mile rides earlier in the week. When I warmed up with a few stretches Saturday morning, my new shorts and jersey felt perfectly broken in.

"Uh-oh, there she is," Bess said. We all looked up as she alerted us. Deirdre was gliding across the parking lot, followed by a couple of guys.

"Looks like her team got matching uniforms too," Ned noted. "Black with blue stripes."

"Mmmm," George said, "black and blue. Sounds

like and omen to me—like maybe DeeDee will crash her hotshot new bike as much as she always crashed the old one."

"Okay, racers, can you gather over here for a minute, please?" Ralph Holman's voice boomed across the parking lot. He was better at speaking through the bullhorn than he'd been at the microphone during the CarboCram the night before. "Just leave your bikes and come in closer," he urged us.

Mr. Holman was standing on the small temporary stage. Next to him stood an impressive, old-fashioned safe. It was black cast iron with shiny brass curlicues and leaf figures in all the corners. A man in a gray uniform stood on the other side of the safe.

All the bikers and the supporters and fans who were there to see the start of the race jostled one another to get a better view of the little stage. I looked around at the other bikers, mostly to check out the competition. I knew most of them, but a few I'd never seen before.

Two of the guys Deirdre had pressed into service were clustered with her, but one had drifted off somewhere. I recognized Malcolm, their truck driver, from school. He was very tall with long brown hair pulled into a ponytail at the back of his neck. I'd never met the other one, but he must have been one of the Jensen brothers. His hair was sun-bleached almost white—at least I assumed it was from the sun.

There were a few people I didn't know at the edge of the crowd who were dressed in racing gear. One of them seemed totally out of place, because he was leaning against a tree and holding on to a bike with fat knobby tires, cantilever brakes on a straight handlebar, and three chain rings. I figured that he couldn't possibly have seen the race route because he had a mountain bike, not a road racer!

"As I'm sure you know, the pledges and donations for this year's Biking for Bucks have already set a record." Mr. Holman's voice pulled my attention back to the stage. "We thought you'd like to see what you're racing for."

Mr. Holman reached over and twirled a long bar that was connected to the center of the antique safe door. The crowd got really quiet. The safe door clicked open slightly. Dramatically he pulled the door open the rest of the way. Everyone gasped. The safe had stacks of money in it—a *lot* of money.

"All the money that you see here has been pledged to the Open Your Heart Fund," Mr. Holman said. "And best of all, it's been pledged in *your* names."

He swept his arm around in front of him, almost as if he were bowing to us.

"Congratulations for everything you've done so far for this wonderful cause," he said, "and for everything you're about to do."

His words made me feel really good. My team came in for a group hug; then we threw our arms up in the air with a cheer.

I led my team through the crowd so we could wish the other five teams a good race. Some of them were kind of scattered around, so we didn't actually get to talk to all of the other competitors.

Deirdre walked up with her team. I recognized one of the guys immediately.

"You're Malcolm Price, right?" I said to her driver. "I'm Nancy Drew."

"I remember you from school," Malcolm said. "This is Thad Jensen."

"That's right," Deirdre said. "You all don't know the Jensen brothers, do you? They're practically cycling professionals. They've won a lot of competitions—all just a warm-up to this race, of course."

Without another word Deirdre turned and walked away. Malcolm and Thad smiled and nodded, but then turned on their heels and trotted off after their queen.

"You don't suppose she's brought in a ringer, do you?" Bess asked. "I mean a real pro—someone we have to worry about."

"So what if she did?" George said. "We can take him. Today we can take anybody!" She put her arm around Bess's shoulder and gave her a good squeeze. "You just keep the truck running. We'll do the rest."

"Did any of you see the man in the red biking shorts?" I asked. "He had a mountain bike and was hanging way back from the crowd, leaning on a tree by the bank."

"I did," Ned said. "Someone should tell him that this is a road race. He's going to have a real handicap against the faster road bikes. There's no real trail-riding in this race."

"I wonder if his whole team is on mountain bikes," George said.

I looked over at the tree where the man in the red shorts had been leaning. His bike was still there, but he was walking toward the stage. Mr. Holman had stepped down into the crowd and was talking to some of the supporters.

Something about that mountain biker bothered me. This guy just didn't seem to fit the picture of an entrant in a charity road race. He also seemed to be a loner with no one hanging with him. So where was the rest of his team?

I watched him pace around the stage for a few minutes. Mr. Holman had moved farther away, meeting and greeting the crowd. The security officer was still onstage, but he was looking over to the side and didn't seem to notice the man in the red shorts circling the area.

While I watched, Red Shorts bounded gracefully up onto the stage and walked right over to the safe. He crouched down in front of the open door, as if he wanted to get a closer look at all the money inside.

I wandered over to get a better view of the action, and I reached the stage just in time to see the security officer in the gray uniform hustle Red Shorts back away from the safe with a friendly smile. Red Shorts jumped backward off the stage without a word and bumped into me as he hurried off. I turned and watched him grab his mountain bike and rush it to the parking lot.

"You too, miss," I heard from behind me. "It's time to get ready for the race. I'm closing up the safe now."

I turned back to the stage and realized the officer was talking to me. "Uh, yes, you're right, Officer . . .

um . . . Rainey," I said, reading his name tag. "You've got quite a job there, protecting all that cash."

Officer Rainey smiled warmly and gave me a brisk professional nod.

"Well, hello there," Mr. Holman greeted me when he stepped back onto the stage. "You're Carson Drew's daughter, aren't you? It's Nancy, right?"

"That's right," I replied.

"I see you're one of our cyclists today," Mr. Holman said, slamming the door shut. "Good luck to you! Better get yourself ready."

As Mr. Holman spoke I watched Red Shorts move through my peripheral vision and then vanish.

I glanced over to the starting line. What I saw shocked me back into reality. Most of the starting riders on the other teams had already pulled their bikes into position. I checked my watch. I'd been so distracted by Red Shorts that I'd missed the call to report. The race would start in twelve minutes.

When I looked back at the stage, Officer Rainey and Mr. Holman were wheeling away the safe on a large dolly. I sprinted back to the parking lot.

"Where's George?" I mumbled to myself. She wasn't at the starting line. In fact I didn't see any of my team anywhere near the line, and the starter was getting his pistol ready.

I found my team still in the parking lot. Everyone was hard at work, unloading spare tubes and tire irons from the truck.

"It was Deirdre, I know it," George snarled as I ran up. "All the tires are flat!"

5

Ready, Set . . . Stop!

Just strip out the tube in the back wheel," Bess ordered. "We've got to get you on the road, George."

"*Both* of George's tires are flat?" I asked, using one of the frame pumps to partially inflate the spare tube.

"Yeah," Ned said with a nod. "And the tires on all the other bikes are too. But you know Bess—she's got plenty of spares."

"Stop talking and pump," Bess said. "We've got to get her out there! We'll worry about the other tires later."

"Evan Jensen was missing from the whole safe presentation, Nancy," George said. "He's probably the one who deflated the tires. But we know Deirdre's *behind* it. We've got to do something about it."

"We don't *really* know that, George," I reminded her. "At this point we have only suspicion, and no proof. Sure I think her team is out to get us. She's always out to get us! But for now we can only stay alert, and see what she might have planned next. And *your* whole focus should be on your ride."

George was really angry—and that was a mixed blessing. A certain amount of heat against Deirdre's team would make her even more fiercely competitive. But I didn't want her to be *so* angry that she'd be distracted from the real goal: bringing home the pledges for the Open Your Heart Fund.

"Just take care of business this morning," Ned told George. "And don't waste your energy thinking about making Deirdre pay."

"Right," I agreed. "She'll make a mistake eventually. She always does. And we'll catch her then. Just be on guard."

With Bess as chief mechanic, we were back in business in six minutes. Bess, Ned, and I helped remount the panniers—the cycle saddlebags—on the rack over George's rear wheel. Then the three of us accompanied George as she walked her bike to the starting line.

"Let's go over it one more time," I suggested as we waited. "This is a relay race, so we'll each take one shift today and one tomorrow. George bikes from ten until noon today. Bess, Ned, and I will be behind you in the truck, George. If you need anything, let us know." I checked her cell phone in its plastic case, which she'd mounted behind her seat.

George flipped on her bike's computer—the same one she had rigged on all our handlebars. Instantly a map of the race course popped onto the screen.

"You're a genius," Ned said, grinning.

"Looks like I have everything I'll need for two hours," she said.

"Well, we're on standby for anything," Bess told her cousin.

"Okay," I continued. "Precisely at noon we will signal you to stop. Remember we've got a GPS on board, so we have to be exact on the times. We'll have one hour to eat."

"I've got the meals all packed, and they're yummy," Bess promised.

"Ned, you'll take the second shift from one until three. Then I'll ride from three to five. We stop exactly at five for the night. I'll do my best to get us to a cool campsite," I added with a grin. "Remember, today's the hard day—tomorrow we each bike only an hour, and the race will be over around noon."

I looked at a map of the race course. It took us

along a set of roads in and around River Heights and some of the neighboring towns. "Maybe we can camp along Swain Lake," I suggested.

"Excellent," Ned said, looking at his map. "We should be able to make that."

"Okay, everyone, let's ride," I said. "George, I know you'll give us a great start." We sent her off with a cheer and she took her place with the other five riders at the starting line.

"Deirdre's sending Thad out first," Bess noted, as Ned and I joined her in the truck.

"I still haven't even seen his brother—the elusive Evan Jensen," I pointed out.

"Deirdre's team truck is ready to roll," Ned said, "so he must be inside already. I wonder who she scheduled to ride next."

"She's not really a sprinter," I answered, "so she's probably going to be up against you. Then Evan will be sprinting the last two hours each day."

"You can take him, Nancy," Bess said. "You're the best. Come on—let's get in the truck. We can see the start from there."

I'm pretty good on a bike, but I knew I'd feel more confident about my ability to do well in this race when I actually saw my competition.

The starter's gun cracked, and the six cyclists burst

away from the line. Thad Jensen bolted ahead of the others, his legs pounding away at the pedals. The six trucks shifted into gear and chugged away after the bikers.

The weather was still perfect. It was about sixty-eight degrees. The sun was masked by fluffy white clouds most of the time, and the air was dry with very little humidity.

Much of the course had been roped off for the race, so we rarely had to contend with any other traffic. Bess settled into an easy cruising speed, and we settled back into our seats for the two-hour leg.

"Have you been able to remember anything more about what happened to you yesterday?" I asked Ned. "Any memory flashes about seeing anyone hanging around the bike rack in the university parking lot, for example?"

"I knew you'd be asking me that, Nancy," Ned said. His arm was resting lightly on my shoulder. We had one of those nice wide trucks, so all three of us could sit up front.

"Last night in bed, I went back over the whole thing in my mind," Ned continued. "And I struck out completely. The only thing I remember for sure is that I definitely pulled the emergency brake."

"Bess and I checked your bike chain, and it looks

like some of the links were filed partway through," I told him. "That plus the car mysteriously rolling into the creek . . . well, it doesn't look good."

"Especially when you add in the flat tires this morning," Bess said.

"Exactly," I agreed. "We need to be on our guard during this race."

We all talked some more about who might have sabotaged our cycle tubes that morning. But, again, no one seemed to have actually witnessed any suspicious behavior.

"George is right," Bess said. "It's got to be Evan Jensen. It's something Deirdre would totally be behind, and Evan was missing in action at the time."

I agreed with her, but didn't say anything more. We could speculate all we wanted, but without proof, we had nothing.

George cycled in her usual masterful form, and by eleven-thirty she and Thad were neck and neck. They jockeyed back and forth for the lead position, but she pulled ahead in the last few minutes. When all the teams stopped for lunch at noon, my team was about fifty yards ahead.

Ned, Bess, and I tumbled out of the truck and raced over to congratulate George. She was lying on her back on a little grassy slope near a wooded area.

Her bike lay next to her, its spokes still turning slowly.

"You did it!" Bess yelled gleefully, parking herself next to George. "We're Number One!"

George nodded and leaned up on her elbows. She looked energized, but ready for a break. While she checked over her bike, Ned stretched, and I helped Bess unload the picnic lunch.

Bess had put together the perfect spread for bike racing. Over a lunch of pasta salad, veggie sandwiches, and granola bars, we plotted our race strategy.

Deirdre's truck was parked about half a football field back down the road from us. We could see the four team members sitting under a large tree in their black-and-blue outfits as they ate. They sprawled on a large blue blanket.

"So Thad gave you a workout," Ned said, "but you took the lead when it counted."

"He's better than he looks," George said. "You'll probably have Deirdre for the next leg. But you can handle her. Just don't give her too much draft. She might know cycling etiquette, but you can be sure she won't use it. Which means she won't be courteous enough to switch off and let you draft her for a while. You know she's a taker, so watch out for her."

"Thanks," Ned said, handing George a sandwich.

"I'll try to hold on to the awesome start you gave us." He finished eating quickly, then he took his bike out onto the road for a couple of warm-up sprints.

"I wish I had a clue about Evan The Ghost Biker," I told Bess and George. I took a bite of my sandwich and suddenly saw Deirdre and her cohorts strolling toward us.

The sun was in my eyes, so I couldn't see their faces all that well at first. Deirdre led the parade of course—and Thad was right behind her.

"Hi, Deirdre," I said, swallowing a wad of unchewed sprout strings. "Hey, Thad, you gave George a good workout!"

"I'm not Thad," the young man said.

"This is Evan," Deirdre said, "Thad's twin."

"Twins, huh? So are you as good as your brother?" I asked. I was just making small talk while my mind was working on something else. I visualized the small medallion I had found under the seat of Ned's car. I didn't even hear Evan's answer, because I was thinking up my next query.

"I have a friend who's really into astrology," I said, when Evan stopped talking. "She says more twins are born under the sign of Gemini than under any other sign. How about you guys?"

"Yeah, that fits us," Thad said, walking up to join the rest of his team. "We're Geminis."

"I've collected a ton of pledges," Deirdre said, butting in to bring the conversation back to her favorite subject: herself. "My team and I are going to break all the records for this event. We're not only going to win in record time, but we're going to set a new high for pledges and money earned."

"Mr. Holman says all the pledges are higher than ever," Bess said.

George stood up so she was eye to eye with Deirdre. "Bess *alone* has brought in—"

"Yes, yes, yes, I'm sure you've all done very nicely," Deirdre interrupted. "But no one else has a supporter as generous as my father. He's agreed to give an extra thousand dollars to the total if we win."

"And we will," Malcolm said, strolling up. "By tomorrow I'll have to rev up the truck just to stay tight with Deirdre. She'll bring us over the finish line while the rest of you are just hitting the edge of town!"

"Deirdre, you're going to be the sprinter?" George said. "Amazing." She plunked back down on the grass.

"I am," Deirdre said. "I've been working with a personal trainer for six months. Nancy, it looks like you'll have some real competition at the finish."

As usual, she didn't wait for a response before walking away. I didn't dare look at the rest of my team. I was using every ounce of willpower I had to keep from whooping with laughter. And I knew that if I looked at Bess and George, I'd see the same tortured expressions on their faces.

Finally I heard Bess giggle into her napkin, and we all lost it.

"Deirdre—the sprinter!" George said, getting up and starting to pace. "There's no way."

"I don't care how good the Jensens are," Bess said. "They are *not* going to beat us."

"Speaking of the Jensens," I said, "did either of you find the fact that they're twins interesting?"

"What do you mean?" Bess asked. "Wait a minute—they're twins!"

"And?" George asked. She stopped pacing.

"Gemini!" Bess exclaimed.

"Remember the medallion I found under Ned's car seat?" I reminded George.

"Proof!" George said.

"If we can connect one of the Jensens to that medallion, then yes, that could be evidence that one of them was in Ned's car," I agreed. "But our first priority is this race. Let's stay focused on that for now. The best thing we can do to show Deirdre's team what we think about their attempts to keep us out of the running—"

"Is to beat them to the finish line!" Bess declared.

"Looks like Mr. Shannon made a safe bet," George added, gathering up some of the leftover food. "His extra thousand dollars is going nowhere."

We had thirteen minutes to get the picnic site cleaned up and get ourselves back on the road. It was crucial that we not waste any time that was legally designated for cycling.

We helped Ned get his bike ready, and he took his place on the edge of the road. While we finished packing the truck, we watched Evan Jensen take his place on the road behind us.

Finally George, Bess, and I piled into the truck. George stretched out on the backseat for a catnap, and Bess and I had the whole wide front seat to ourselves.

"Let's move," I said. "I'd like to get our rig on the road before Deirdre's truck."

"I hear you," Bess said, turning the ignition.

There was nothing but the click of the key in the slot.

I watched as she turned the key again. Nothing.

"Hey, what's happening up there?" George

mumbled drowsily from the back. "Let's hit the road."

"It's no good," Bess said, taking the key out of the ignition slot. She slumped back in her seat. "It's not going to start."

6

Charlie's Got a Secret

"**W**hat's wrong, Bess?" I asked.

"Something serious," Bess answered, as she hopped down out of the truck.

She hurried to the front and lifted the truck hood. George and I joined her. I peered inside, although I wouldn't know what was wrong from just looking in there. Bess was definitely the mechanic on this team.

"I was right," Bess said immediately. "The distributor cap is missing."

Bess is amazing when it comes to cars—or anything mechanical, for that matter. She might look like someone who wouldn't know a distributor cap from a hubcap. But she does. If she says the distributor cap is missing, you can bet that's exactly the problem.

"Not the kind of thing you have spares of on hand, I'll bet," I said. I pulled out my cell phone and pushed the fifth button. Everyone laughs when they discover that I have Charlie Adams on speed dial. But it has always been a good idea. And today it was a *great* idea.

"We were lucky," I told the others. "Charlie was in the garage. He'll be here right away." I checked my watch. "Okay, it's thirty seconds to one o'clock. It's time to count down for Ned. Don't tell him about the truck."

"Shouldn't he know what's going on?" Bess asked.

"No. It's not necessary right now," I answered. "Not when he's about to kick off his leg of the race. His focus needs to be totally on outcycling Evan Jensen. I don't want to distract him from that."

"There's nothing he can do about a missing distributor cap anyway," George added.

"Exactly," I agreed. "If Charlie gets here pretty quickly, we can get on the road right away, and Ned won't even notice that we had any trouble. If we get stuck out here longer, we can call him later and tell him."

We ran to the edge of the road where Ned sat on his bike, keeping his balance by leaning down on his left foot.

"Nineteen . . . eighteen . . . seventeen . . . ," I called out, watching the second hand on my watch.

My temples throbbed as I watched him lean down over the handlebars. Suddenly something occurred to me. Was the stolen distributor cap a prank played by Deirdre's team? If they could do that right under our eyes, could they have done something to Ned's bike, too?

And what about his broken chain the day before, and his car in the creek? Prank or crime? Dirty trick or assault? If they could get away with that, what else could they think up?

"Ten . . . nine . . . eight . . ."

I shook off any concern I had. He'd just checked out his bike from top to bottom—it was good to go. And Bess had even given her stamp of approval. That's all anyone needed. As if he were reading my mind, Ned flashed me a winning grin and a thumbs up.

"Three . . . two . . . one."

He kicked off and cycled away without a backward look. Bess, George, and I stepped out into the road and sent him off with an exhilarating cheer.

We heard an echoing cheer behind us. I turned around just in time to see Evan Jensen barreling up the road. I pushed Bess and George onto the grass and leaped after them. Fifty yards back, Deirdre, Malcolm, and Thad were still cheering as they ran to their truck.

"That jerk didn't even swerve to miss us!" George said.

With a roar Deirdre's truck peeled by. Deirdre, Malcolm, and Thad laughed and waved as they raced by.

"They know our truck won't start," George grumbled. "Because *they* sabotaged it!"

"It's going to take Charlie at least fifteen minutes to get here," I said. "I can't stand to just sit and wait. I'm going to check over my bike."

"Good idea," George said. "If they could mess with the truck, they could get to the bikes—which they already did this morning, actually." She lay back on the grass and looked at the cloudy sky. "I can't wait until tomorrow morning," she muttered. "I'm going to grind that Thad Jensen into the road!"

I got my bike off the rack and began going over every inch of it to make sure it was as ready as I was to take on Deirdre's team.

"Bess, why don't you call race headquarters and tell them what's happened," I suggested. "When they check our GPS, they'll wonder why we're sitting here."

Bess punched the number into her cell phone and started talking almost immediately.

"And tell them we'll be using the shortcut to catch up with Ned," I added.

Bess nodded at me as she spoke into the phone. When she was finished, she flipped it shut and reported the conversation.

"Everything's okay," she said. "I told the woman Charlie is on his way, and that we'll be back on the road as soon as possible. She said there's no need to check back in when we get going—they'll pick it up on the GPS. She also said it will be okay to take shortcuts with the truck in order to catch up to Ned."

"Okay, I have just one little question," George said, with a sly grin. "Which member of Deirdre's team stole our distributor cap? We certainly had it when we parked here. So the theft *had* to have happened sometime while we were here. And there was only one set of visitors—Deirdre and her gang."

"*Gang* is definitely the right word," I groused. "And I didn't see anyone else around the truck—or even this area."

"But Deirdre's team was with us the whole time," Bess said. "They walked up, we talked to them, and they left."

"Except for one member," I said. I went back over our postlunch encounter with the other team. "Deirdre

63

and the twins walked up by themselves. Malcolm wasn't with them then."

"You're right, Nancy!" Bess said. "Malcolm's their driver. I remember now. I noticed he wasn't with them, and I figured he must have been checking out their truck."

"Looks like he was checking out *our* truck instead," George said.

"We don't really know that for sure," Bess said.

"Well, it's a pretty good guess," George said. "We're the only two teams camped out here. I'm really getting steamed about all these pranks." George began pacing again. She looked like she was going to explode with anger.

"I agree that they're pretty close to crossing the line," I told her. "In fact I think they crossed it when they rolled Ned's car into the creek—which I figure they probably did. But unless we can find Malcolm's fingerprints all over the hood of our truck, we're not going to be able to tie him conclusively to the stolen cap. And I have a feeling he's too smart to leave his prints behind."

"But now a bunch of different things have happened," Bess pointed out. "Doesn't that help us make a case against them? If we add up all these different incidents, isn't that enough suspicious behavior to at least have the police question them about it?"

"It *does* make a difference," I agreed. "And when the race is over, we should definitely consider doing something official about all these dirty tricks. But for now let's put the Open Your Heart Fund first."

"Done," George and Bess pledged simultaneously.

We all clasped right hands and pumped them into the air. Our mission was clear.

I went back to fine-tuning my bike. Bess continued checking the backup cycle, and George finished collecting the lunch trash.

Charlie Adams rolled up with his road-service truck just as I was finishing my cycle check. He was always a welcome sight. He waved to us all as he drove off the road and over to our truck.

"Hey, Nancy. So, you're having some trouble, huh?" he asked with a warm smile.

"I'm sure glad you can help us out, Charlie," I said. "We really need to catch up with Ned as soon as possible. I don't like having him so far ahead of us. You brought us a new distributor cap that's guaranteed to help us win the Biking for Bucks, I bet."

"Well, now, I don't know about that," he said. "But I brought several, just in case. We'll find one that works—I can promise you that."

Charlie and Bess went to the front of the truck. George and I walked my bike to the back and secured it on the rack. Then I walked around to rejoin Charlie and Bess—and to pick Charlie's brain. George followed my lead.

Bess was trying to fit a cap on the distributor, but it didn't seem to be the right size. Charlie held two more caps in his hand. When he saw me coming, he ducked his head under the hood as if to escape.

"So what's the latest word on the race, Charlie?" I asked. "I'm sure you've heard about everything that's been going on. Anything happening I should know about?"

He pulled his head out and looked at me, and then he quickly looked away. He rolled his eyes around and looked over at George, and then down at the ground. He seemed to be nervous and uncomfortable.

"Well, yes, there *is* something—but I really can't say," he answered. He kept looking at the ground.

Bess popped out from under the hood. "This one doesn't fit," she announced. "Let me have the others."

Charlie handed her the other two caps. He gave me a weak smile, then turned away to watch Bess.

"Everyone's talking about our team being Number One, I'll bet," George said.

"Mmmm-hmmm," Charlie mumbled.

"Charlie," I said in my softest, most unthreatening voice. "What is it that you can't tell us?"

"I can't do it this time, Nancy," Charlie said. "This is really big—the guy that told me made me swear not to say anything." His voice echoed slightly, because he wouldn't take his head out from under the truck hood.

"But, Charlie, you know I won't tell anyone," I nudged. "There's nothing more sacred than the bond of confidentiality between a detective and her informant. I wouldn't dare let anyone know you'd entrusted me with confidential information. Besides I've never betrayed your trust before—and I'm certainly not going to start now."

"What about *them*?" Charlie said. He was obviously referring to Bess and George, but acted as if they weren't even there.

"They're not only part of my cycling team," I told him, "they're also trusted members of my detecting team. They are just as obligated as I am to keep your confidence."

"Well, okay," he said in a low voice. "But this is big, Nancy, really big. The guy that told me is in the know and everything."

I wanted to reach down into his throat with both hands and pull the words out. But I forced myself to stay calm. Sometimes getting Charlie to tell me something is like trying to get a cat out from under the bed for a trip to the vet.

"It's okay," I said in a low voice. "What happened?"

I held my breath so long waiting for Charlie's answer, I could feel a warm flush in my cheeks.

"It's the money," Charlie finally said. "The Biking for Bucks pledges." He shook his head, and his eyes widened into almost perfect circles.

"What about the money?" I prompted, although I had a feeling that I knew what he was going to say.

"It's gone," he said. "It's all gone."

Shifting My Gears

G one!" Bess shouted, breaking the quiet tension of the previous few minutes. "What happened to it?"

"Someone stole it, that's what," Charlie said. He took a deep breath, and let it out with a sigh. Then his words began pouring out.

"When the money was put back into the vault," he said, "the guards were required to recount it. When they opened the locked box, all they found was shredded newspaper. The cash was gone—it had just disappeared!"

"I remember the old-fashioned safe that the money was in," I said. "Mr. Holman opened the safe to show us all the money."

"That's right," Charlie said. "I was there. I wanted

69

to see the beginning of the race. And I knew they were going to be showing the money."

"We're talking about a *lot* of money," George said. "Thousands—tens of thousands."

"That was their first mistake," he asserted. "You show all that money to people, and someone's bound to get greedy."

"As a matter of fact, there was a guy with a mountain bike—," I began.

"Are you talking about the one in the red shorts?" Bess interrupted.

"Right," I said. "Did you see him, Charlie? Do you know who he is?"

"I don't remember seeing him," Charlie said. "But he wouldn't have been in this race on a mountain bike, would he?"

"He wasn't one of the starters," George said, "but he could be on one of the teams. We just don't know yet."

"When Mr. Holman left the stage after he'd opened the safe, the guy in the red shorts hopped right up there," I told Charlie. "He was showing a lot of interest in the money, and was hanging around the open safe."

"Where was the security guy when he got up there?" Charlie asked.

"Officer Rainey was distracted and didn't see him at first. When he finally did spot the guy, Rainey chased him off the stage—but I couldn't believe that guy was up there in the first place."

"Did Mr. Holman see all this?" Charlie asked. "He wouldn't have like it one bit."

"I don't know," I answered. "He climbed back onstage shortly after that. That's when he and Officer Rainey wheeled the safe offstage. The race started soon after."

"That's right," Charlie said. "I saw them push that thing away. The safe looked pretty heavy."

"And the thieves didn't take the safe," I said quietly, mostly to myself. I was trying to picture how it happened. "They just took the money."

"But when did they take it?" Bess asked.

"That's the big question," Charlie said. "When they opened the safe to recount the money, there was nothing but newspaper."

"All those stacks of cash," Bess said, shaking her head in disbelief. She was still trying the new caps.

"So it happened between the time they wheeled off the safe, and when they reopened it to count." I was still thinking aloud.

Charlie started stepping back and forth from one

foot to the other, as if he were getting nervous about telling us what happened.

"The cops are keeping a really tight lid on this," Charlie said, looking around as if there might be eavesdroppers around him. "Remember you promised not to tell anyone I told you about it."

"I'm sure they're trying to find the money before the race is over," I pointed out. "They don't want the riders and their supporters to be discouraged about the whole point of this event: the money they're raising for charity."

"The Open Your Heart Fund, yeah," Charlie said, nodding. "It'd be a real shame if that money's gone for good."

"How did you find out about it?" I asked.

"I got called to tow in a car with an overheated water pump," he answered. "And it happened to belong to someone working at the race. Hey, it was that Rainey guy—the one who'd been up on the stage with Mr. Holman. No wonder he was frantic."

"Does Officer Rainey work for the bank?" I asked. "Or is he someone hired by the race organizers—a private security service?"

"I don't know," Charlie answered. "I've seen him around, though."

"I got it!" Bess yelled triumphantly. "This cap works." She raced around and jumped into the truck. I breathed a big sigh when I heard the engine start up.

"I've got to get back to town," Charlie said. "Good luck, you guys. You're my favorite team!" He started his truck and waved. "Don't forget. You heard *nothing* from me about the missing money!" he shouted out the window as he pulled away.

"Let's go," George said, jumping into the backseat.

"I can't," I told them. "We have to change our strategy. Right now."

Bess and George got out of the truck and walked over to where I stood. As I worked out the plan, I started to talk.

"Look, it was sometime during the last three hours that the money was discovered stolen. I figure the police put roadblocks up on every street leading away from River Heights, and they've got to have officers watching the river, too."

"What are you saying?" Bess asked.

"If someone was trying to get out of town with that money, they'd have been caught by now, and the money would be back in the bank."

"And Charlie would probably have heard about it," George said.

"Exactly," I agreed. "Whoever stole it is smart enough to wait and not try to escape until they think they can get away with it."

"Like at night?" Bess reasoned.

"That's what I'm thinking," I said.

"So the money is probably still around town somewhere," George concluded.

"Which means I've got a chance to find it and get it back into the right hands before the race is over," I said. "I have to try."

"Wait a minute," George said. "Are you saying you're pulling out of the race?"

"I have to," I said. "I'll ride our spare bike back to town. And you two and Ned can keep going in the race. Bess has to use my bike because it has the GPS on it."

"Nancy, we'll help with the case too," Bess said. That was just like my friend—always wanting to help.

"I've been saying all day that we have to stay focused on the race," I said. "And we *still* do. There's a rule about having no more than three riders on a team. But there's no rule about who drives the truck or who does the cycling. We packed the backup bike in case of an emergency. This definitely qualifies."

"So you want me to bike *and* drive the truck?" Bess asked, confused.

"You can all bike, and you can all take turns driving the truck. Bess, you take my leg this afternoon after Ned. Then if I'm not back to ride by morning, we'll set up a new schedule for tomorrow so that the strongest one sprints the last leg."

"But *you're* the strongest," Bess said. "We'll need you."

"I'll try to be back before tomorrow morning," I said. "Until then each of you has to do your best. The point is to make our pledges."

"Are you sure you don't want our help with the case?" George said. "I'll give up the cycling if you think you could use a hand."

This was a lot for George to offer. She's been involved in sports practically since she started walking, and she's one of the greatest competitors I've ever known. It was really cool for her to be willing to give that up to help me solve a case. But it wasn't necessary. I smiled and shook my head.

"What about Ned?" Bess asked. "Don't you think we'd better call him now and tell him we've changed the plan?"

"Or we could wait until the three o'clock changeover," George offered.

"I'd better call him," I decided. "I really don't want to disrupt his focus now. But if he sees you riding up to take over at three o'clock instead of me, Bess, he'll be even more disrupted. His first thought will be that something happened to me."

"Good point," George said. "Plus it's one forty-five now. He's figured out that we're not nearby, so he's probably already wondering if something's happened. It'll ease his mind just to hear your voice and know what's going on."

"You call him," Bess said. "We'll get the backup bike down—I'd better give it a quick once-over."

"I'll drive the truck the rest of this leg, so Bess can rest up," George said. "Find out exactly where Ned is, so we can catch up with him."

The racecourse took us on a very convoluted path. There were lots of twists and turns, hairpin curves, and blind hills. It was designed to be a difficult course to follow, and thus harder to race. By using straight country roads, George could meet up with Ned more quickly.

I took out my cell phone and pushed the speed-dial button that connected me to the cell phone behind Ned's seat.

George had rigged up the racer cell phone with a remote button attached to the handlebar, and a one-unit earpiece/mouthpiece that fit into our helmets.

When the phone rang, we wouldn't have to reach behind the seat and pull it out; we'd just push the remote button, and the caller's voice would fill our helmets. The mouthpiece was in our helmet straps, so we didn't have to handle that either. She modeled the whole system after the one that racecar drivers use.

I was happy to hear Ned's voice. At least one member of our team was on track. It took me only a few minutes to give him the full story and to tell him my plan.

"And you'll be okay?" he asked. I could hear the concern in his voice, and it gave me a warm, comfortable feeling.

"I'll be fine. And I'll be even better when I know that money's safe and secure back where it belongs."

"So I'll be changing over to Bess at three o'clock," he said. "I'll miss seeing your big blue eyes."

Sometimes Ned knows just the right thing to say. "Yeah, well, Bess has big blue eyes too," I reminded him.

"That's right . . . she does." He laughed. "Okay, then."

"You sound pretty chipper. Where are you?" I pulled out a map of the route.

"I'm approaching the hills near Berryville."

"Perfect! The truck will meet you on the other side. And Bess might be able to get you all to Swain Lake by five o'clock. Or at least close to it—maybe by the river."

"Excellent. Take care of yourself. Get the case solved and the money back and meet us at Swain Lake for dinner."

"Hmmmm . . . that's a tall order! I'll either be there or call in. You take care too."

I hated to break the connection, but we both had major business to attend to. Images of gazing at moonlight on the water with Ned had to be filed away until later.

"The backup bike is totally clean," Bess said, wheeling my cycle over. "It's a hybrid, too, so it will not only take you over roads. You can also ride it on any weird detours you might have to follow. I've got your backpack and snacks in the panniers. I also threw in your jeans and sweater in case you don't have time to go home and change."

I thanked Bess and showed George where Ned was on the map, and where I told him he could hook up with the truck. Then I pulled on my helmet and gloves.

"Okay, team, go get 'em," I said as I mounted my bike.

"You too," Bess called back as she climbed in the truck's passenger seat.

George and I each pulled out onto the road. George turned left, and I turned right.

8

Feathering My Brakes

I rode the straight chute back to town, cutting across lawns and through alleys. It was only a few miles that way. I headed for downtown and the finish line, at the intersection of Highland Boulevard and Main Street.

I briefly considered stopping off at home to change clothes, because I didn't want to attract too much attention to myself. I've lived in River Heights all my life, and a lot of people here know me for one reason or another. Even people who didn't know me would notice someone riding around town in race clothes on race day. I didn't want anyone to know that I had dropped out of the race—mainly because I didn't want anyone to know *why*.

Just then I remembered that Bess had packed my sweater and jeans in the panniers—so I decided to ride over to Dad's office downtown to freshen up instead of going all the way home.

I biked from the edge of town to Highland Boulevard. My dad's law office is on Highland. Sometimes it's open on Saturday, but that day it was closed because of the race, and because Dad was out of town.

I had my own key, of course. I unlocked the back door and took my bike inside. I spent a few minutes washing up. I left my racing clothes on, but pulled my jeans and sweater over them. I was a little warm, but a bit of sweat never hurt anyone.

Grabbing my backpack, I locked up Dad's office, and left. I walked up Highland to the corner at Main Street. This was not only the start and finish line for Biking for Bucks, it was also where Mr. Holman had shown us the pledge money in the safe.

At first I hung out casually near the minipark, *pretending* to read the paper in the newsbox, but really watching the activity in front of the bank across the street. A few people walked around, but not many. Most of the shops were closed because of the race. With the streets blocked off, there wasn't much point in stores being open.

I wanted to check out the area around the start and finish line, but that was impossible. Two uniformed police officers and at least three recognizable detectives in plain clothes were still looking for clues around the makeshift stage and bleachers that had been constructed for the weekend. Clearly, neither the money nor the thief had been found yet.

I crossed the street and walked past the bank. I wasn't surprised to find that it was closed. It would have been even if there hadn't been a theft, because it always closes at noon on Saturday, and it was already three o'clock.

No one seemed to recognize me or pay any attention to me. I strolled past the bank and looked in the window. There was a lot of activity inside. Tellers counted money in drawers, and officers questioned security guards. Others just sat, checking papers, which I guessed were probably lists of pledges—pledges of money that had vanished.

In the corner Mr. Holman and Officer Rainey stood on either side of the old-fashioned safe. Its door was open, just like it had been that morning before the race. Except this time the safe was empty.

I walked back to the other side of Main Street and into the minipark. As far as activity was concerned, the park was the exact opposite of the bank. A couple of fat bumblebees lazily nosed their way into some petunias, and a plump red cardinal sat in the middle of a birdbath. He wasn't even flapping his wings to pretend he was actually bathing. He was just zoned out, tail-deep in the water.

A weathered bench offered a perfect view of the front door of the bank. I really wanted to talk to Officer Rainey, since he was the one who had been watching the money. But how was I going to get to him?

I sat for a while, watching the cardinal sitting like a fat red rock in the birdbath. My mind was busy with images of the safe, of Mr. Holman and Officer Rainey, and of the man in the red shorts.

For a moment I considered going over to police headquarters. My main source there is Chief McGinnis. He isn't exactly a friend, but he's more than just an acquaintance. The best word to describe him is *colleague*. We often find ourselves working on the same case, although we definitely have different methods—and often different results.

As I was debating with myself about the merits of checking in with Chief McGinnis, I was joined on the park bench by a friend.

"Luther!" I greeted him. "Lend me some of your wisdom."

I'm always happy to spend a few minutes with Luther, because I always learn something when I do. And sometimes I don't realize I learned anything until later.

"Hello, Nancy," Luther said with his thin little smile. "Now why am I not surprised to find you down here instead of sprinting around the cycling course?"

"Because you know me so well?" I guessed, smiling. Even though Luther is old enough to be my father, we always treat each other like good friends.

"So tell me," I continued, "why don't you seem that surprised to see me out of the race?" I asked.

"Because a major crime's been committed on the same day," Luther replied, his blue eyes shining.

"You've heard about the stolen pledge money," I said, nodding.

"I have, and I figured I'd find you down here where the action is. And besides, it's a nice day to be in the park."

"Well, it seemed like the right place to be—but now I'm not so sure. I want to talk to Ralph Holman or the security officer who was guarding the pledges this morning. But it looks as if the police have them tied up inside the bank."

"Not literally, I hope!" Luther said with another smile.

I couldn't help but smile back. "They might as well be. They're standing guard over an empty safe."

"You know . . . ," Luther began.

I love it when he begins a sentence with "You know," because it's usually something I *don't* know at all.

"You know," he repeated, "this whole theft reminds me of the original River Heights Heist."

I know the legend of course. Everyone who lives here has heard it a million times. But Luther's definitely the expert on this town and knows all the little sidebars that haven't necessarily made the history books.

"You know about the Rackham Gang of course," he said.

"Before the settlement even had a name"—I paraphrased the brochure from the River Heights Welcome Board—"a steamer arrived with a big load of cash to exchange for Mahoney anvils. But the word got out, and the Rackham Gang stole the money."

"You get an A-plus for common knowledge," Luther said. "*Now* tell me some of the not-so-common facts."

"Okay, let's see. I remember you showing me exactly where the original heist took place," I said. It had been pretty exciting, actually. I could almost feel the history of the place come alive as he described the legendary theft. It was as if River Heights had its own pirate tale.

"What else," I said. "Oh, yeah—when Lucia Gonsalvo found that gold coin last year and thought it was from a sunken treasure ship, you identified it as part of the Rackham Gang loot."

"Very good," Luther said.

"So what am I missing?" I asked. "Why are we talking about the Rackham Gang?"

"Well, as I said, it seems to me that the theft that took place across the street this morning is like the one by the Rackham Gang a century ago."

"How so?"

"The Rackhams seemed to disappear into thin air. They were spotted before the heist, but nobody saw them in town after the theft."

"You told me they escaped on the Muskoka. They had a boat waiting downstream."

"That's right," Luther said. "The sheriff staked out the river, but unless you plant someone every couple of yards or so, there's no way to cover every possible place to cast off a boat—especially at night. The

Rackham Gang hid out until after dark. Then they escaped down the Muskoka with the loot."

"Are you saying you think today's thief escaped the same way?"

"I'm sure you'll figure it out," Luther said, patting my shoulder as he stood. "You're a clever one."

As I watched Luther walk down the path, the bright red cardinal shook off his soggy feathers and flew away. I watched the bird until it vanished in the afternoon sunlight, and I thought about my conversation with Luther.

Suddenly I flashed back on the scene at the starting line that morning, when a stranger in shorts the color of a cardinal's feathers seemed to vanish into thin air.

"I've *got* to talk to that security man," I told myself. "He saw Red Shorts too—in fact, he warned him away from the safe. He must have put him on an interrogation list."

I went back across the street to the bank and peeked through the window again. The activity inside had dulled some, and the empty safe stood unguarded. Most of the people were gone. I couldn't see either Ralph Holman or Officer Rainey.

I walked casually back around to Highland Boulevard and down to the alley that ran along the back of the bank. A couple of police cars blocked the opposite ends of the alley. One unmarked black car was parked halfway between, near the bank's back door.

I didn't see any people in the alley, but I expected that someone would be guarding the bank's back door. I hoped it was one of the River Heights policemen that I knew—someone who would answer my questions about the theft. I've worked with a few of the officers in town on past cases—strictly unofficially, of course. I really hoped it would be Chief McGinnis.

I sidled past the car that blocked the entrance to the alley. It was four thirty, and the bank building blocked the direct sun. The alley was a patchwork quilt of wavy dashes of bright reflected light and blotchy panther black shadows.

As I moved from the heat of the sun, a chill rippled across my shoulders. No one stood outside the bank door. I placed my ear against the cool metal door, but I couldn't hear anything from the other side.

The door had no knob or lever. A swipe card slot was embedded in the wall next to it. That meant that employees were given magnetized identification cards.

I reached up and gave the door just the slightest

push with my fingertips. My breath stuck in my throat as the door slowly moved forward—and a voice shouted behind me.

"Nancy Drew!"

9

Red Light, Green Light

Nancy! Don't tell me you've taken up bank robbery!"

I recognized the voice.

"Chief McGinnis," I said. I turned around and gave him my most winning smile. I had mixed feelings about running into him this way. I was glad because I usually could get some information from him—but I wasn't happy that he'd found me sneaking around the back door of the bank. He gets upset with me when he thinks I'm butting into his territory.

I decided the best defense is a good offense.

"I'm so glad I found you—I've been looking for you everywhere. I finally figured out that you might be back here."

Well . . . it wasn't a total lie, right?

"Re-a-lly," he said, breaking the word into three parts. I had given him my best smile, but he gave me his best *frown*—and he had the bushy dark eyebrows to emphasize it. "It looks more like you're breaking and entering to me."

"Wow," I said. "You've got this really difficult case to solve, lots on your mind, but you can still come up with a great spontaneous one-liner! Incredible." I smiled again.

He didn't say anything, but I could tell by his expression that he was pleased with my compliment. He seemed to relax just a little bit. Within seconds, though, he was frowning again.

"What case are you talking about?" he asked. "And how did you find out about it?"

"How did I find out that the pledge money was stolen? Actually, I've heard it around town—from more than one person. I was hoping you could tell me the real story."

"No, I cannot," he said firmly, stepping between me and the bank door. He's half a foot taller than I am, and his middle is *much* bigger around than his chest. He made an excellent—and successful—barrier.

"Because you *won't* tell me, or because you *can't*?"

I asked. "Don't you have anything on the case yet? No suspects, no leads?"

"No information for you—that's what I've got!" he said firmly.

"How about Officer Rainey?" I suggested. "He should be a good source of information. What did he say when you interrogated him?"

"I can't believe you," Chief McGinnis said, shaking his head. "Although after all these years, I shouldn't be surprised that you know so much about what's going on. Why are you here? *Really.*"

"I'm here to talk to you, and to talk to Officer Rainey and Ralph Holman—*really,*" I answered.

"Well, you've talked to me, and we're through talking. One out of three ain't bad. I'm sorry, you can't talk to Officer Rainey, and you *especially* can't talk to Holman."

"Why especially not Mr. Holman?"

"This interview is over, Nancy. Come on, I'll walk you back up the alley."

He rested his hand lightly on my back and gently pushed me away from the bank. As we walked along the narrow alley, I persisted in trying to get a crumb of info out of him.

"Just tell me this," I asked. "Did you hire Officer Rainey? I mean, was he provided by the River

Heights Police Department? Or did the bank hire him? Or the race organizers?"

"He's from a private firm," Chief McGinnis answered. "Hired by the Biking for Bucks board of directors."

"Mrs. Mahoney is the chairwoman of that board. My dad is one of the directors."

"That's right," Chief McGinnis replied.

While we were talking, I was being hustled down the alley. He didn't exactly nudge me, but the way he walked made me keep going in that direction. It was either that or walk straight into the brick wall. I felt like I was a sheep being herded by one of those dogs that are bred to keep the strays in line.

"And if I'm not mistaken, Ralph Holman is *treasurer* of the Biking for Bucks board," I said. "That makes sense, of course—he's a banker. Of course he was also in charge of the money during the race—and during the theft. What did he say about the robbery?"

"Not much so far," Chief McGinnis answered. "But we hope to change that."

"Are you saying he's a suspect?"

"I'm sayin' only what I'm sayin'." Chief McGinnis has a tendency to talk that way once in a while. Sometimes I think he's seen too many old cops-and-robbers movies.

"And you've talked to Officer Rainey, too, I assume, since he was hired to keep just such a disaster from happening," I guessed.

"Of course," he answered.

"Did he mention a guy in red shorts? He hustled this man away from the safe when it was being displayed at the starting line. A guy with a mountain bike."

"I don't remember."

This was one of the most frustrating things about dealing with Chief McGinnis. He and I often have different ideas about how to solve a case. For example, if I had interrogated the one security officer guarding the cash before it was stolen, I'd remember every word he said.

"He had on biking shorts, so I thought he was on one of the racing teams."

"Okay, correct me if I'm wrong—and I'm sure you will," Chief McGinnis continued. "There were a lot of people running around this morning. In shorts. With bikes."

"But this guy was different. He had this mountain bike, for one thing. And I'd never seen him around town before."

"There are several people in the race from out of town. And contrary to public opinion, you actually don't know *everyone*." For the first time in our conversation, Chief McGinnis really smiled.

We were halfway to the end of the alley when I heard people talking behind us. I turned just in time to see two officers in normal clothes escorting Ralph Holman out of the bank and into the unmarked black car.

"He's handcuffed!" I whispered to Chief McGinnis. "Mr. Holman is handcuffed!"

"That's right, he is," the chief said. "Now get out of here—and keep your mouth shut about this. If it gets out to the public before we release it, I'll know who leaked it, and it will be the last piece of information that you will ever get from me about any case I'm working on. Ever! Do you understand? Don't think I'm kidding about this. I mean it."

"Is Mr. Holman being arrested for the theft?" I asked. "Just tell me that much."

"Nancy, you already know more than you're supposed to. Do us both a favor. Let's end this conversation while we're still friends."

I couldn't resist just one more question as Chief McGinnis left me where the alley emptied into the street.

"I assume you set up roadblocks and guards at all the boat landings, right?" I called out to his retreating back.

He didn't answer me or turn around, but he

nodded and gave me a thumbs-up. Then he hurried back to the unmarked car.

I watched them drive away—the two plainclothes-men, Chief McGinnis, and their prisoner, Ralph Holman.

I walked around to the front of the bank and searched the ground near the race's start/finish line. There was nothing to clue me in on what had happened that morning. If there had been any evidence still there, the herd of investigators I'd seen swarming around earlier had gathered it all up.

I visualized the interaction between Mr. Holman, Officer Rainey, and the man in the red shorts. Then I walked to the tree where Red Shorts had been leaning when I first saw him. I crouched at the foot of the tree and brushed at the thick grass and weeds. There in the dirt was a perfect print of a bike tire— a thick mountain bike tire. The print was about six inches long. And it was precisely in the spot where Red Shorts had leaned his bike against the tree.

I reached in my backpack for my pocketknife and sliced a border in the dirt around the print. Then I looked around and spied a poster lying on the side-walk announcing the race.

I wedged the edge of the poster into the cut I had

made in the dirt. Then, very carefully, I wiggled the cardboard under the tire print, working my way up the whole length. Using the poster as a tray, I lifted the block of dirt up out of the ground.

Carrying my treasure from under the tree, I headed quickly back down Highland Avenue to Dad's law office. I put the tire print on my dad's desk and photographed it with the instant camera he keeps in the credenza behind his desk.

When I had a picture that showed the tire pattern clearly, I tucked the photo into my backpack. Then I eased the dirt block into a plastic bag and placed it on a shelf in his office refrigerator. I put a sign in front of it saying PLEASE DO NOT DISTURB and signed my name.

Then I planned my next move.

I really wanted to locate Officer Rainey. If I could just talk to him, I could ask him about Red Shorts. And now I had even more to ask him about—Ralph Holman. It was six twenty, and I was tired. I also needed to call my team, as promised. I decided I could do a much better job of that over a latte.

I grabbed my bike, locked up Dad's office again, and headed for Susie's Read & Feed, a bookstore and café on River Street. It's one of my favorite hangouts. It's a great bookstore, with new and used books. And it's also a charming café. I locked my bike in the rack outside Susie's and went in.

"Hey, Nancy, welcome," Susie Lin called to me from the back of the café. She's the owner.

"Wait a minute," Susie said as she joined me. I was looking at the large bulletin board in the café, covered with job offers and other ads. "Aren't you supposed to be tooling around the countryside right now? I thought you were in the race this weekend."

"I'm on a short break," I said. "Bess is riding this leg." I really didn't want anyone to know what I was doing—not even Susie.

"Bess? Well, good for her! But you . . . you're on a break. What's up?"

"Nothing, really. Just couldn't race without having one of your muffins first."

"It's apple-nut today," Susie told me, pointing to the chalkboard propped up over the cash register. Susie always writes the day's specials on it in her distinctive no-nonsense block letters. She makes incredible muffins.

"So what can I get you?"

"Mmmm, at least one muffin," I answered. "And a latte."

"You want the muffin warmed up?" Susie asked.

"Absolutely."

"Take a seat—I'll be right back."

I looked around. There were several serious book buyers probing the shelves, but the Saturday evening regulars hadn't strolled in yet, so I had a nice choice of tables.

I took a seat at a small round table with chipped blue paint. I plopped my backpack into the chair next to me and dug into it for my phone. As I was looking down, two hairy legs walked past my table and stood in front of the chalkboard with their calves toward me.

I couldn't control the shudder that ran through my body when I saw who had wandered in. I didn't see his face, but I'd recognize those red biking shorts anywhere.

10

Spinning My Wheels

The man in the red shorts stood with his back to me for a few more minutes studying Susie's chalkboard. Finally I heard his voice for the first time. It was low and scratchy.

"I'll have a veggie wrap and an Americano," he said. "Extra mustard on the wrap."

"For here or to go?" Susie asked.

"Here, I guess," he said.

"It'll be just a few minutes," Susie said. "Have a seat anywhere."

The man turned and started toward the bookcases—the biology section—but I stopped him with a question.

"Excuse me—I saw you at the starting line of the

bike race this morning," I said. "How come you're not out on the course? Aren't you on one of the cycling teams?"

I held my breath when he looked at me because he could have been asking me the exact same question. But my gamble paid off. Apparently he didn't recognize me without my racing clothes. To him I was just a patron of Susie's.

"Uh, no," he answered. "I was just there to . . . uh . . . I was—do I know you? Haven't I seen you around somewhere?"

I held my breath while he stammered out his questions. Maybe my first impression was wrong. Maybe he *did* recognize me.

"No, I don't think so," I answered quickly. "You might recognize me from this morning, though, hanging around the start of the race. Like I said, that's where I saw you."

He narrowed his eyes as I spoke. His shoulders seemed to tense up as he studied me. Did he remember bumping into me as he was chased offstage away from the safe?

"Oh, yeah, that must be it," he finally said. He took a deep breath and appeared to relax.

He was kind of seedy-looking up close. If he'd shaved that morning, he hadn't done a very good job. Or maybe he was trying to grow a beard, and it was in that stage where it just made the lower half of his face look dirty. His black jersey was faded, and fraying threads hung from the ends of his sleeves. His sneakers were caked with muddy clumps.

"I'm sure I saw you with a bike this morning," I persisted. "That must have been why I thought you were on one of the teams. I'm a big fan. That's my road racer out there."

Red Shorts looked out the window at my bike in the rack. "Pretty cool," he said.

"I have your order ready," Susie said, coming up behind Red Shorts with a tray. "Where would you like to sit?"

"You can join me if you want," I suggested. "I love to talk about bikes."

Susie gave me an odd look—almost a frown, but not quite. I could tell from her expression that she thought Red Shorts and I were an odd match. She probably wondered why I was even talking to him, let alone inviting him to sit at my table. She tilted her head slightly. Red Shorts couldn't see her because she was still behind him.

I raised my eyebrow and shook my head slightly. She's known me for a long time and knows I'm a detective, so I took a shot and hoped she'd understand my gesture.

I could almost see her adding up the facts—Nancy's left the race, Nancy's talking to this weird guy, Nancy must be on a case. I knew she'd gotten the message when she smiled and spoke up.

"Good idea," she said, putting Red Shorts's sandwich and coffee in front of an empty chair at my table, and then handing me my muffin and latte. "Enjoy."

She left quickly to go back to the kitchen, her straight hair flipping from side to side. Red Shorts paused for a minute, then pulled out the chair and sat down.

"My name's Nancy," I said, holding out my hand.

I decided not to tell him my last name. I'd never seen him before this morning, but I'm often surprised to learn that people who've never met me have still heard of me.

"Jasper," he responded.

He held out a thin, long-fingered, grubby hand. He barely clasped mine, then took his hand back and wiped it on his napkin. I wished he'd done that before he touched me. His hand felt oily, sort of slimy.

"Is that your first name or your last?" I asked. I couldn't tell and didn't know whether to call him "Mr. Jasper" or not.

"Just Jasper," he said, taking a huge slurp of steaming Americano.

He looked out the window again. "So that's yours, huh? I'm surprised *you're* not in the race. You could make some real time on that thing. It's pretty slick."

"Yeah, well, all the teams were filled by the time I considered it," I said, sipping my latte and breaking off a piece of my muffin. "What about you? How come you're not out there?"

He didn't answer at first, opting to take an enormous bite out of his wrap. "This is really good," he said. He wasn't exactly talking to me. He was just announcing it into the air.

He whipped his head around and yelled at Susie. "Fix me another one of these wraps, okay?" he yelled. "Man, I'm hungry."

"You got it," Susie called back.

A group of six chattering college-student-types came through the door and took a long table with benches next to the far wall. I didn't know any of them, and I was relieved about that. I didn't want anyone recognizing me and asking me about my team in front of Jasper.

"I don't have a road bike," Jasper said, finally coming back to my question. "Or any bike, for that matter. This morning I had a mountain bike. But there aren't too many mountains around here." He grinned.

"We've got a lot of rough terrain though," I said. "A mountain bike would be really handy along the river and over some of the hills around River Heights. Do you live here in town?"

"Well, that bike's not mine anyway," Jasper said, ignoring my question.

"It isn't?"

"Nah, it's my brother's. I haven't had a bike since I was a kid. I borrowed the mountain bike from him 'cause I was going to trek downriver for the weekend. Do you like snakes? I do. I was going down to pick some up. Thought I'd start a little business."

"You must have had to cancel the trip, I guess, or you wouldn't be here," I concluded. "So what happened?"

"Eh, my brother needed the bike back. He had to go someplace after the race started and his car broke down. I might get me one of my own though. That bike's got a real good feel to it. And you're right, it does great along the river. So much of that land is still so wild."

"It's wonderful, isn't it?" I said. "It's so cool that the town is keeping it undeveloped. It's great for hiking and riding."

"Mmmmmph," Jasper said, stuffing the rest of his wrap down his throat.

"Okay, I'm taking this one with me," he told Susie when she delivered his second sandwich. He glugged the rest of his coffee and jumped up from his chair.

I watched closely as he paid for his meal. He used grubby old bills wadded in a small change purse. Then he nodded once at me, grabbed his bag of food from Susie at the counter, and hurried out of the café. He shuffled across the street and out of sight.

I went outside to watch him, although I was pretending to check my bike chain. Crouched behind the spokes, I had a good view. A block away he got into a beat-up tan sedan and quickly drove up Main Street. The car wobbled in the back, as if the shock absorbers were shot.

I stood up. It would do no good to follow him on my bike. Even if I could keep up with him, every time he looked in the rearview mirror, it'd be pretty obvious that I was tailing him. So I went back inside to pay my bill—even though I hadn't even had a chance to eat my muffin.

"Tell me the truth," Susie said, her voice low. She looked from side to side while she talked, as if to make sure no one was overhearing our conversation. "You're on a case, right? Can you tell me about it?"

"Let's just say I'm looking into some things," I

answered. "Do you know anything about that guy? Does he live in town?"

"I've only seen him a couple of times," Susie said. "I think he lives somewhere on the river. I try not to listen to my customers' conversations, but I can't help hearing sometimes. He was in here once before with someone, and they were planning to go down the river to Rocky Edge and catch snakes."

"Right—he told me he wants to start a snake business, whatever that means. Yuck."

"*Yuck* is definitely the word," Susie said. "I stopped listening when I heard that."

Susie handed me my change and I left. I knew I had to call my team. By this time they'd set up camp and were probably eating dinner. I wondered how Bess had done on the last leg of today's course. I missed being in the race, and I wished I'd been out there streaking through the loopbacks with the others. But there was no question about what my priority should be. All the racing these two days would be for nothing if the stolen pledge money wasn't recovered.

I also knew that I *had* to talk to Officer Rainey. My encounter with Jasper Red Shorts was inconclusive. His whole attitude and his behavior in Susie's café had been so casual and laid back. It was hard to believe that he'd committed a major theft just hours earlier.

I didn't expect the thief to be out of town yet. Luther made a lot of sense when he compared today's robbery with the historic one by the Rackham Gang. Whoever stole the money would be crazy to try to leave town before dark. And Chief McGinnis reinforced that when he confirmed that there were roadblocks to the main exit routes.

But nighttime is another matter—especially along the water, where there's no way to cover every inch of the riverbank. Susie said she thought that Jasper lived somewhere on the river. He'd probably know all sorts of inlets and hidden spots along the bank where he could launch a boat and get away with a stolen bag of money.

Officer Rainey could definitely be the key. He would surely remember the only person in the crowd who dared to jump onstage and practically stick his hands in the safe.

There must be some way . . . Mrs. Mahoney! She's the chairwoman of the Biking for Bucks board of directors, and they hired Officer Rainey. She'd have some idea where I could find him. I also wanted to get her thoughts on why Mr. Holman had been arrested. I'd talk to her first, and then call my team and give them a full update.

I jumped on my bike and headed straight for Mrs. Mahoney's home. I knew she would see me without an appointment. My father has been her attorney for as long as I can remember—since her husband, Cornelius, was alive. And I have helped her occasionally fend off the con men who have preyed on her since she became a rich widow.

The Mahoney home is in the most elegant area of town, on Bluff Street. Mrs. Mahoney answered the door herself, dressed in navy blue slacks and a creamy white sweater.

"Oh, Nancy, dear, forgive me for greeting you like this," she said. "Our butler is out of town visiting his sick aunt."

That was typical of Mrs. Mahoney. *She* apologized to *me* because the butler didn't open the door for me and she had to. Dad says that she is very up to date in a lot of ways. But in other aspects—such as manners and behavior—she is definitely from a different era.

"Oh dear, Nancy, you've heard, haven't you? What are we going to do? You'll help, won't you? How nice to see you, by the way. But aren't you supposed to be biking?"

She looked at her watch. "Oh, it's evening, isn't it? The teams are resting now. But you're not, are you? You're trying to find our missing pledge money. I suppose you've heard about Ralph Holman. How lovely of you to work on this case in the middle of your racing."

In less than two minutes, she had summed up my whole day.

"Yes, I am on the case, Mrs. Mahoney. I've already talked to Chief McGinnis and some other possible witnesses. But I'm trying to find a source who might be able to open up the case a bit more, and I'm coming up dry. I came here because I know you can help me."

"Of course, Nancy. Anything I can do, of course. What is it? What do you need?"

"I need to talk to the security man you hired to supplement the bank's security force and watch the pledge money. His name is Officer Rainey. He's from a private firm, but I don't know which one. If you can tell me that, I can track him down. I really think he's key to the investigation, and I'm eager to interview him. Can you give me the name of his firm?"

"I can do better than that, my dear. I can give you Officer Rainey himself. He's in the conservatory right now."

11

My Midnight Sprint

Here?" I said. "**Officer** Rainey is here?" I couldn't believe my ears. Sometimes a detective digs and probes and studies and researches. And sometimes she just lucks out.

"Yes," Mrs. Mahoney said with a warm smile. "He is giving me his report about the theft and how it happened. Come join us for tea. Three heads are better than two."

She led me to one of my favorite rooms in River Heights. No matter what time of the year, this room could transport you to paradise. It was a two-story round room capped with a large dome. All the walls and the dome were made completely of large panes of glass set in copper frames. The copper had weathered to a rich, pale greenish gray. Most of the glass was very old, with wavy patterns, and even bubbles in it.

"Officer Rainey, you are in for a real treat," she called out as we entered the room.

She led me through the thousands of blossoming flowers and dozens of tall trees and other potted plants that thrived in the room. We skirted around small tea tables and chairs to the main table in the middle of the room.

"It's Nancy Drew!" Mrs. Mahoney said to Officer Rainey. I was a little embarrassed by her enthusiasm. I had hoped to keep a lower profile with this man, but then I didn't expect to be escorted right up to him either. Sometimes you have to take the bad with the good.

Mrs. Mahoney sat near the tea service. I sat down on one side of her, and Officer Rainey—who had politely stood as we approached the table—sat down on her other side. I liked that. He was directly across from me and I would be able to study his face as we talked. He still wore his security service uniform.

"Hello, Officer Rainey," I said. "I'm so happy to find you. I've been wanting to talk to you from the minute I heard about this morning's robbery." I knew there would be no point in beating around the bush.

Officer Rainey's face was a study in human expressions. He seemed to go from shock, to puzzlement, to anger, to embarrassment, to resignation—all in a split second.

"But how could you have known about—," he began.

"Oh, Nancy knows everything," Mrs. Mahoney said in a very matter of fact way. She didn't even look up as she poured the tea.

"Oh, no," I said quickly. "No, I don't. That's exactly why I wanted to talk to you, Officer Rainey."

I sat back in my chair as I had my first sip of tea. I recognized the flavor immediately. It was Darjeeling from India. It's my favorite, because it tastes like chocolate to me.

"She even knows that Ralph Holman has been arrested," Mrs. Mahoney said, passing a silver plate of small sandwiches neatly arranged on an embroidered linen napkin. Another two-tiered silver dish held cookies and tiny blueberry tarts.

"Nancy's here in a purely professional capacity," Mrs. Mahoney continued, "although she is a personal friend of mine. She and you are colleagues, you see. Nancy is also an investigator."

"I see," Officer Rainey said. He still seemed puzzled. He took a bite of roast beef sandwich and a sip of tea.

"I don't really know you as part of any particular team of uniformed or undercover detectives. So I assume your interest in the case is unofficial?"

"Nancy has solved many cases that our very own police department had trouble with," Mrs. Mahoney said. She leaned over and spoke in a low voice, as if she were telling him a secret. "Believe me, she knows what she's doing."

"And why is it exactly that you wanted to talk to me?" he said, after smiling briefly at Mrs. Mahoney. "You realize that I won't be able to tell you any details as long as the official investigation is ongoing."

"Of course," I replied after swallowing. The roast beef sandwich was delicious—I'd had nothing since lunch except a bite of muffin. "I wouldn't think of asking you to compromise your own work on the case," I continued. "My main interest is in a man that I watched you chase off the stage this morning. He was a biker in red shorts who had jumped up to get a really close look at the money in the safe."

Officer Rainey sipped his tea again and seemed to be thinking. Actually he seemed to be sizing me up, as if he were wondering how much he should tell me.

"Yes, I remember him very well," Officer Rainey finally said. "I assume he's a rider on one of the bike teams."

"Didn't you think it was strange that he just hopped

onto the stage like that?" I asked. "You were looking to the side talking to someone, but you were still very close to the safe. He didn't seem to be worried about that at all. He just jumped up there anyway."

Officer Rainey smiled at me, but it was one of those weird smiles. The smile that means "Don't bother your pretty little head about something you're too young or too inexperienced or not smart enough to understand." Yuck.

"Well, sometimes sports competitors get really pumped up about a game or a race or whatever," he said, as if he were teaching me one of the premier rules of life. "Their enthusiasm and exuberance make them do silly things. I figured he was just getting a close look at all that money to remind himself why he was going out there to win."

"We've had more money pledged this year than ever before," Mrs. Mahoney said. She nodded several times and popped a sugar-coated almond cookie into her mouth.

"Well, that's just it," I told them. "I've talked to that man myself. His name is Jasper, and he isn't actually one of the racers. He had a mountain bike—"

"That certainly wouldn't do," Mrs. Mahoney interrupted. "You need a good road racer for this course."

"Exactly," I said. "And he was never a part of any of the teams or intending to race at all. So perhaps he was interested in the money for another reason."

"I see what you're saying now," Officer Rainey said. He put his teacup down and leaned forward, with his elbows on the lace tablecloth. "And I'm not only surprised. I'm really grateful to you. I was told he was one of the bikers."

"Who told you that?" I asked.

"He did," Officer Rainey said, throwing his hands up in the air. "I tracked him down this afternoon as soon as I knew the money was gone. Of course I was as concerned as you were about his jumping up on the stage. I have to tell you that I'm also very embarrassed that it happened while I was there—that it happened on my watch." The worried look returned to his face.

"Now, now," Mrs. Mahoney said, patting his arm. "There's enough blame for what happened to go around. The goal now is to get that money back and put the wretch who stole it behind bars."

"Well, thank you, but I'm going to feel this way until I personally find the culprit who's responsible," Officer Rainey said. "It should never have happened while I was in charge of the safe, and the only way to restore my good reputation is to bring the thief to justice."

"What about Ralph Holman?" I asked. "The

River Heights police seem to think he's guilty of something. What are the charges, do you know?"

"Oh, I don't believe for a minute that he had anything to do with the robbery," Mrs. Mahoney said. "I've known Ralph all my life. Yes, I know he's had some financial problems lately. Haven't we all! But it's simply not like him to do something illegal to make up for his losses. I'm sure they will never be able to indict him for stealing the Biking for Bucks pledge money. That's just more of Chief McGinnis's grandstanding: Arrest someone immediately. Never mind whether you have the actual criminal or not."

"You said you tracked down this Jasper guy," I said to Officer Rainey. "Does he live in town? I don't remember seeing him before."

"Not exactly," Officer Rainey said. "I think he lives south of River Heights. I don't know where—when I talked to him, he was still hanging around town."

"And you still considered him a suspect after talking to him?" I asked.

"Absolutely," he answered. "And you don't need to worry about the case any longer. I'll find him, believe me. And when I do, I'll find that money and get it back in the safe."

"Good luck," I said, standing up. "Thank you so

much, Mrs. Mahoney. Please don't get up. I can see myself out."

"Thank you for coming, Nancy," she said. "It's always delightful to see you."

As I left the conservatory, I could hear the two of them whispering about me and about the case.

I slowly wheeled my bike away from the Mahoney mansion. Luther's voice echoed in my mind, telling me to follow the river. Then I heard the voices of Susie saying that Jasper Red Shorts lived somewhere on the river, and Officer Rainey telling me he thought Jasper lived south of River Heights. Hmmm.

The closest international airport was in the state capital, downriver. It would be a great place to lose yourself or get out of the country if you'd just ripped off tens of thousands of dollars from a charity. . . .

I was just three blocks away from the river. When I got there I turned south. Most of the land for miles along the river had been set aside as wilderness, public trails, and parks. So there weren't that many residents down that way. If Jasper lived south along the river, I'd find him—and I'd check out every house and shack along the way if I had to.

I also planned to check for hidden boat-launching sites and keep an eye out for anyone cruising the river that night. I had the photo of the mountain bike tire pattern, and that would be a big help. If I was lucky, I'd find the same pattern along the muddy bank and just follow the trail from there.

I had plenty to tell Bess, George, and Ned now. I reached behind my saddle and pulled out the cell phone. I didn't know whether they'd be within calling range or not, so I was excited when Ned answered on the first ring.

"Nancy! It's about time!" he said. "What's happening? Where are you? What are you doing?"

"I'm heading south along the river," I said. "How far did you get on the course?"

"We didn't make it to Swain Lake," he said. "But Bess was outstanding. We lost some ground . . . not much. We're only behind Deirdre's team by about twenty minutes. George was finally able to hack into the GPS system on her computer, so we know exactly where Deirdre's team is camping."

"And where are you now?"

"We're on the river near Rocky Edge."

"I'm heading that way. I'll be there in about an hour."

"Okay, be quiet when you come in," Ned warned me. "Deirdre's team isn't far away, and we don't want them to know you're coming."

"Good idea," I said. I hung up, grateful that I could stop and see my friends—and most of all, get another change of clothes and a chance to rest.

When I neared Rocky Edge, I stopped pedaling and coasted the rest of the way down the bank. I felt a shot of much-needed adrenaline and warm feelings just seeing the small campfire my friends had built.

We all talked at once for the first several minutes—but we did so quietly. We knew our voices would carry to campsites farther up the river. And we certainly didn't put it past Deirdre or her gang to plant a spy nearby to listen in on our conversations.

"Bess was fantastic," George told me. "She kept really close to Deirdre. I am so primed to tear up the course tomorrow morning. I'll cover Thad Jensen with mud as I fly back up this river!"

"What have you found out, Nancy?" Ned asked. "Tell us what's happening."

I filled them in on my day: talking to Luther, being caught by Chief McGinnis prowling around the back door of the bank, watching Mr. Holman being taken away in handcuffs, digging up the mountain bike tire track, talking to Red Shorts at Susie's, and interviewing Officer Rainey at Mrs. Mahoney's.

"So you didn't get much accomplished, right?" George said with a smile.

"Yeah, right," I said, smirking back.

"Looks like Red Shorts is the guy, don't you think?" Bess asked.

"He seems to be," I answered. "But I don't know . . . he sure didn't act like someone planning a major escape. That bothers me. And how does Mr. Holman fit in? Is he calling the shots? Are they accomplices? I have a feeling I'm missing something important, but I just can't put my finger on it."

"Are you sure you don't want us to work with you, and we'll all bring in the bad guy together?" Ned added. "We might be able to help."

"I know, but I still feel strongly that there's a lot at stake here as far as the race is concerned. I plan to solve this case—and in the meantime our team needs to fulfill its pledges."

"And grind Deirdre and the boys into the ground once and for all," George added. Always competitive, that George.

"But if you don't find the money, it doesn't matter *who* wins the race," Bess pointed out.

"I'll find the money," I insisted. "You win the race!"

When I said that, I got another rush of adrenaline. A real urgency flooded over me. I had to make good on that promise.

I quickly put on fresh biking shorts and a jersey.

Then I pulled on a hoodie and workout pants over the bike clothes. The late-night air had turned chilly.

"I packed a sandwich, snacks, an energy drink, and a couple more energy bars in your panniers," Bess said.

"Thanks," I said. "And thanks most of all for bringing extra biking clothes!"

We all clasped hands and pumped them in the air. There was no cheer this time in case the nearby wilderness hid human ears. With hugs all around, and a kiss for Ned, I was on my way again. It was eleven fifteen.

I stayed off the main bike trail—the one that the racers would be using the next day. Instead I took the old path that ran between the public trail and the river.

The old path was hidden by undergrowth and weeds. It was a little rougher than the trail, but nothing the backup bike and I couldn't handle. And I figured that someone on a mountain bike would be more likely to use the older path. I also didn't want to call any attention to myself, since I knew other bikers might be camping along the riverbank and might wonder whose bike headlight was coming at them.

At first both the darkness ahead and the glare of my headlight were startling when I pulled away from the bright flames of the campfire. But my eyes gradually got accustomed to both extremes. I watched the path ahead carefully.

I had ridden just a little over three miles when I saw it in the river bank mud—the perfect squiggles of a mountain bike tire track.

12

A Dangerous Switch

I stopped my bike, got out the photograph of Jasper's bike tire tread, and brought it close to my bike's headlight beam. It was an exact match to the one on the old path.

A cool shiver cascaded down my spine, causing goose bumps to pop up under the sleeves of my hoodie. I jumped back on my cycle and followed the mountain bike trail. It was patchy, and once in a while it would phase out altogether for a few yards. But then I'd pick it up again in my headlight. Jasper's bike had definitely traveled this same path. That is, Jasper's *brother's* bike had traveled this same path.

Another wave of chills. Jasper's brother, I reminded myself. Jasper told me he was going to use the bike this weekend, but then his brother needed it back because . . . because . . . his brother's car had broken down after the race started.

"Yikes!" I said out loud, and then clapped my hand over my mouth, hoping no one had heard me. Of course!

Charlie Adams told us that he had been on a service call to fix Officer Rainey's water pump right after the race had started. And Jasper told me that his brother needed the mountain bike back *right after the race began because his car had broken down*. Jasper never told me his full name. Could his last name be Rainey?

I pulled the brakes and stopped my bike. I dropped my left foot down to lean on for support. I needed a few moments to follow my trail of thought, instead of the bike trail.

In my mind I went over every word that I could remember of my conversation with Officer Rainey and Mrs. Mahoney while we had tea in the conservatory.

Officer Rainey had told me at first that he wasn't concerned about Jasper jumping up on the stage that morning because he thought he was merely an eager competitor. Was that why he smiled when he hustled Jasper back off the stage? Was it a friendly smile from a public servant? Or a smile of recognition for a brother?

Seemed too simple. There's more, I told myself. Think.

What was it Officer Rainey said about talking to Jasper later? Oh, yes—he said he didn't know where Jasper lived, because when he had interviewed him that afternoon, Jasper was still hanging around town.

But wait a minute—he also thanked me for telling him that Jasper was not one of the racers.

Of *course*! That's what I'd been trying to figure out for the last hour. Officer Rainey was lying! If Jasper was still hanging around in the afternoon, Rainey already *knew* he wasn't in the race. Rainey either lied when he said he thought that Jasper was one of the racers, or when he said he talked to Jasper that afternoon. Either way, Rainey hadn't been honest. And it didn't matter whether he was lying to protect his criminal brother or lying to protect his own criminal skin. He had some major explaining to do.

I got back in the saddle and picked up the trail of mountain bike treads in the mud. After a few more miles the tracks veered off the old path and down a rugged hill toward a large cluster of trees and bushes. A DEAD END sign was posted at the top of the hill.

I turned off my headlight, pulled my bike off the path, and hid it in a large bramble bush. I took my backpack out of one of the panniers and checked the contents. I emptied out the comb and lip balm and other stuff I didn't need. I didn't know how long I'd be hiking, so I wanted to keep the pack as light as possible.

I took my cell phone, pen and notebook, pocketknife, energy bars, and penlight. Then I pushed my bike, my helmet, and the other stuff I was dumping under the bramble bush. Unless someone was looking for it, it wouldn't be spotted.

Quietly I started hiking down the hill, following the trail of Jasper's brother's mountain bike. There was just enough moonlight to see where I was going. When I got to the edge of the river, the bike trail ended—and I saw something moving gently ahead. A decrepit fishing boat bumped at the end of a very short pier.

I ducked behind a fallen tree and watched the area for a few minutes. There was nothing—no sound, except the lapping water and the bumping boat. No one in sight. I waited a few more minutes to muster my courage, and also to plot an escape route. Then I darted straight for the little pier.

I crept quickly across the creaky planks and gazed into the boat. There was a small cabin in the middle of the deck, but it was mostly windows. I crouched to look through the glass. No one was on board—at least until *I* stepped off the pier onto the deck.

The boat was pretty run down, and I saw nothing

that would identify the owner. I stepped inside the cabin, which meant I walked down three short steps. Pulling the penlight from my backpack, I swung the beam around the small room.

A built-in bench along one wall had an old mattress stretched over it. One rickety-looking wooden kitchen chair and a couple of barstools made up the rest of the furniture. A hot plate, an electric popcorn popper, and assorted dishes—both clean and dirty— filled the counter and sink in one back corner. Next to that was a tiny closet full of canned goods with a fishy-smelling canvas deck cover wadded on its floor. The other corner in the back contained a door leading to the teeniest bathroom I'd ever seen—even smaller than the ones on planes.

There was trash piled everywhere in the main room—stacks of newspapers, food wrappers, empty bags—but nothing that looked as if it could be holding a wad of stolen cash. There were no closets. I checked the one cupboard under the sink. There were some pretty disgusting things under there, but no money.

I went to the bench that ran along the wall. I really didn't want to touch the mattress, so I gently kicked the front of the bench. Hollow. I went to the end and pushed at the corners. The top corner was firm, but the bottom gave a little.

There was no handle, but I wiggled my finger under the wood and tugged. Half the wooden front pulled up like a door hinged at the top. Inside was a set of panniers, a little larger than the ones my team had. They looked like they could serve as saddlebags for a mountain bike.

I eased the bags out onto the floor. They were bulky and heavy. Sure enough, when I opened them up, I found neatly wrapped stacks of cash.

Thinking quickly, I stuffed the money into my backpack. Then I grabbed a handful of newspapers from the ones scattered around the floor, and shoved them into the panniers. I would give Rainey a taste of his own medicine.

I jammed the panniers back into the hidden cupboard and dropped the door down. Then I closed the door, so that it looked exactly the way it had when I found it.

Finally I stood up and swung the backpack full of money onto my back. My only thought was to get off the boat. My heart was beating so fast I felt like it would pop right out of my chest. I couldn't even hear the boat bumping against the pier anymore, because the pulse in my temples drowned out all other noises.

Well, *almost* all noises.

The sound of clattering metal landing on the deck

outside the little cabin rang out into the night. The boat dipped hard to the right, and I had to take a step to keep my balance. Something had been thrown onto the boat deck, and it sounded like it might have been the mountain bike.

I jumped up and raced for the closet. Another unsettling dip to the right was followed by the sound of footsteps. Someone had stepped onto the deck!

I ducked into the closet and pulled the door shut. As I locked myself in the tiny room, the boat motor chugged to life.

13

Rattled!

The light in the room was dim, and the door was only inches from my face. I felt the boat lurch to the right and start to move fast. An arc of light washed over my left shoulder. I looked up and saw a small vent opening at the top of the closet wall. The moonlight was filtering through a screen mesh. That meant we were heading south.

I was pretty sure that there was no one else on the boat but the person who was piloting it, so I knew I could move around and change positions without being heard. It was definitely close quarters, but there was a *little* room for movement.

I was really worried about a couple of things. One, that the pilot would come into the cabin and try to get into the closet. Or two, that he would come into the cabin to check the money. Either way I was in trouble. I assumed it would be a *he,* because I was thinking it would be either Jasper or Officer Rainey.

What would I do or say if I was discovered? If it was Officer Rainey, I could pretend that I was happy to see him and treat him as if I thought he was tracking the bad guy just the way I was. If Jasper discovered me, my response would have to be different. Either way, I'd have to pretend I knew nothing about the money on board, and try to distract whomever it was from getting close to my backpack. My goal would be to get away as fast as I could—with the money.

While I was working on a possible scenario with Jasper as the pilot, I slumped down onto the canvas piled on the closet floor. My legs ached, so even sitting on the smelly deck cover was better than standing one more minute. I suddenly realized how tired I was. I'd been going nearly full strength for a long time, and it was finally catching up with me. I pulled an energy bar out of my backpack and chomped it down in four bites. Then I washed it down with a couple of slugs of water. It tasted so good!

My eyelids felt really heavy, but every time I closed my eyes, I saw the image of the old road moving between the spokes of my front bike wheel. I could feel my legs pumping the wheels again, and hear the hum of the tire buzzing in my ears.

Soon the boat seemed to settle into the river current as it chugged further away from the pier. It was just an old fishing boat, but it didn't feel as if it were moving very fast. I figured the pilot was maneuvering at about half-speed to keep the noise level down.

The boat seemed to rock from side to side as it chugged along, and I scrunched further down into the canvas. At first I had trouble keeping my eyes open. Then I had trouble opening them at all. Finally I no longer heard the motor or smelled the fishy canvas. The only sensation I had was rocking from side to side. . . .

THUNK!

A loud noise vibrated through the boat and jolted me out of my sleepy fog. I shot straight up to my feet and shook my head. There was just a sliver of moonlight slicing through the small screened opening at the top of the closet. I checked my watch. Four o'clock!

My thoughts tumbled. I wasn't just coming out of a daydream. I'd slept for over an hour!

My heart started fluttering again, and I took a couple of deep breaths to clear my head. Footsteps thumped around the deck to the cabin door, and then down the three steps into the room.

I stood perfectly still, my ears straining to hear. There was a shuffling noise, and then a creak. And then it was still.

There was no sound for almost fifteen minutes. Then snoring and snuffling sounds filled the air. Someone was snoring! I realized that the pilot must have fallen asleep on the mattress across the room.

I hadn't even thought of this possibility. I ditched all the plans I'd made and sketched out a new one.

After considering different courses of action, I decided to risk leaving the boat while the person slept. If it was Officer Rainey, I would still go with my original plan—telling him that we were two colleagues hot on the trail of the bad guy. If it was Jasper, I'd have to make something up on the spot.

I figured that trying to sneak off the boat gave me at least a chance of leaving without discovery. All other options *began* with my being discovered.

I made myself wait another fifteen minutes or so before doing anything. The snoring had continued without any pause, and it was definitely loud enough to cover my exit noises.

Okay, I told myself at last. Here we go. . . .

I unlocked the door and opened it slightly. Even I couldn't hear the latch click above the snoring. I moved behind the door for a moment, fully hidden from the person sleeping on the mattress.

The snoring continued, so I stepped out into the room. The sleeper was Officer Rainey, still in his uniform. I crept across the small room, fully aware of the dangerous cargo I carried on my back.

Up the three steps, across the deck, and over to the pier. So far, so good. I stepped carefully off the boat, trying to cause as little motion as possible. I could still hear the snores as I vaulted across the pier and onto land. I noticed there was another boat tied to the pier. It was a high-end speedboat, perfect for a rapid escape downriver.

The moon was nearly gone. I needed to get out of there as quickly as possible. I didn't really know *exactly* where I was, but I figured I had at least a couple hours' hike back to where I had hidden my bike.

I jogged quietly up the pier, my legs keeping time with my pounding pulse.

"Aaaaaschwhewww!" The loudest, longest sneeze I'd ever heard punctuated the stillness. When I looked around, the light flicked on in the boat's cabin. Through the window I could see Rainey stretch and stand up. Then he walked toward the steps leading up on deck.

For a minute I couldn't move. It was like one of those dreams in which you *want* to run, but you can't. I looked around for a hiding place.

I saw a shed halfway up the hill and raced for it.

135

The slapping of my full pack against my back spurred me on. I darted into the shabby wooden shed and closed the door.

Through a crack between the boards I watched Rainey pad around the deck of the boat. He had brought some kind of food with him—I was too far away to tell what it was exactly. He sat on a box and began eating.

Just watching him eat made me hungry again. For a second I dreamed about Hannah's banana bread. Then I forced myself to focus on the present.

I knew I didn't dare leave, or he'd see me. I stood there watching, waiting, my senses picking up on my immediate environment. The inside of the shed smelled really weird. It was a musty smell, sort of earthy, combined with another scent. I couldn't put my finger on what it was.

I could hear Rainey's footsteps on the boat deck. He seemed restless, not content to just sit on the box. As I watched, he'd get up and pace around every few minutes.

Then I heard another sound—something shuffling around behind me. My whole body jumped. I wasn't alone in the shed.

No light penetrated the little structure at all. The moon was low in the west, and the sun hadn't begun to rise yet.

At first I was afraid to turn on my penlight—afraid Rainey would see the light moving inside the shed. But after a few more shuffling, slithering sounds, I didn't have any choice. I had to have light.

I swung my backpack around to get at the front pocket, and this brought on a flurry of noises. It was as if someone was sweeping a large broom across the floor. I unzipped the pocket. More sounds.

I turned my back to the door to try to shield what I was about to do from Rainey. Then I flashed my light onto the floor at my feet. I moved the arc of the light beam out around the floor.

I was sharing the shed with dozens of snakes! All sizes and several varieties coiled and crept away from the light. Yuck! I could feel the packets of cash in my backpack as I pressed backward into the door, trying to get as far away from the slithering creatures as possible.

My mind flashed on what Jasper had told me about wanting to start a snake business, and what Susie had overheard him say about catching snakes.

The snakes I saw in the light were the garden variety of nonpoisonous snakes. But they were still not something I'd choose to share a shed with at night—or even in the daytime, for that matter. Which was worse, I wondered: being trapped in the shed with snakes, or letting Rainey know I was there?

I sent Rainey a strong telepathic message to leave. Jump in the speedboat, I pleaded silently. Go! Head for the city. Head for Brazil. Anywhere. Just get out of here!

I craned my head around, nervous about turning my back on the slithering assembly. Either Rainey had picked up on my plea, or his restlessness had come to a head. He went down into the cabin and came back out, carrying the panniers. He obviously didn't know his saddlebags were full of newspapers.

"Come on, come on," I whispered. I was reaching the height of restlessness myself. I *had* to get out of that shed!

I swept the light across the floor again, startling my roommates back into their coils. Then I turned to watch Rainey, my fingers firmly gripping the door handle.

Rainey turned off the light in the cabin of the fishing boat, threw the panniers into the speedboat, and jumped in after them.

The sound of the speedboat motor zooming into work mode didn't mask the new sound I heard behind me. It wasn't the garden variety snake kind of sound this time. This noise I'd heard only at zoos, and once when I was on a case in the California desert. Dry, hollow rattles echoed from the far corner of the shed.

As the speedboat zoomed away, I yanked open the door, dove outside, and slammed the door behind me. Then I raced down to the pier, and tumbled onto the old fishing boat. The key was dangling in the ignition. Yes! I turned on the engine and steered the boat away from the pier. The faint, rosy yellow glow of dawn was just beginning to seep over the trees on my right.

It seemed to take a lot longer to get back up river to the pier where the fishing boat had first been docked. This was mainly because I wasn't sure exactly where it was, and because it was so small and secluded that I ran into several dead ends before I finally found it.

I moored the boat and went back up the hill to my bike, which was still safely hidden under the brambles. I took off my backpack and fell onto the ground. Lying back on the dewy grass felt *wonderful!* It had been a long time since I'd been able to lie down. I stretched and ate some fruit that I found in my panniers. I had only a few snacks left, and I knew I'd need some later.

I had a bottle and a half of water left, so I allowed myself one-quarter of a bottle. It was positively the *best* water I'd ever tasted in my life.

With a new wave of energy I went back to work. I took the money out of my backpack and stuffed it into my panniers, followed by my folded empty backpack.

While I worked, I noticed the DEAD END sign I'd seen so many hours earlier when I'd first arrived at this hill. I startled myself with a loud giggle. Being trapped in a dark shed full of snakes is bad enough. But when the silence is broken by rattling noises, the words *dead end* take on a whole new meaning.

I stood, stretched again, and checked my watch. It was a little after eight. I figured I was about three hours from town, so it would take at least that long to return. Realistically I knew it might take longer because the energy I felt was mostly mental and emotional. Physically I was exhausted. I was determined, though, to get the money back to River Heights.

I knew it wouldn't do any good to call my team from where I was; I was still in the wilderness area, too far from town for cell reception. So I strapped on my helmet, hopped on my bike, and started for home. My goal was clear: to get the money back in the bank. Preferably before the race was over.

The sun was warm on my bike. I kept myself going by keeping my mind busy. I visualized my team, and could feel their support and encouragement even though they didn't know where I was. I thought about Mrs. Mahoney, Mr. Holman, and all the other supporters and people who'd pledged money for the race. I thought about my dad and Hannah, and how proud they'd be that I'd solved the case. And most of all, I thought about the people who would benefit from the Open Your Heart Fund.

Periodically I dipped into my snacks, and I stopped at a couple of streams to rehydrate and splash water on my face.

At last I reached the road that was the final leg of the racecourse. I knew there was no stopping now. As I approached the edge of town I rewarded myself with the last of my water and my final energy bar.

I felt a rush of adrenaline when I pulled onto Main Street. Ahead I could see the bleachers full of fans. My dad and Hannah were in the front row, right on the finish line. Just seeing that Dad had made it back in time gave me a new burst of energy, and the whole weekend flashed through my mind in quick images. I barreled on, pumped by one final, thunderous cheer.

I grinned and raised my arms for the crowd.

"Nancy! Nancy!" Familiar voices chanted my name as I coasted along. Mrs. Mahoney and Mr. Holman—apparently released from jail—rushed up the street to greet me.

How did they know I had the money? I wondered. Why was everyone so thrilled? I haven't even told them about it yet. But then I noticed the ribbon trailing back from my shoulders—finish-line tape!

14

And the Winner Is?

Drew! No *way*!" I heard Deirdre's voice shouting behind me. She whammed her bike right into mine, and we both spilled to the pavement.

She jumped to her feet and headed toward me. Her usually pale face was beet red with rage.

"Nancy Drew!" Mr. Holman walked up, beating Deirdre to the punch—literally. He helped me to my feet.

"There's no way you won this race, Drew," Deirdre shouted, as she pushed her way through the cheering throng beginning to crowd around me. "I've been so far ahead of you I haven't even seen you! You *couldn't* have caught up with *and* passed me without my knowing it. You had to have taken a shortcut. You totally cheated."

"Not exactly," I said, righting my bike and removing the panniers. "I veered off course all right, but it was hardly a *short*cut."

"I think you'd better explain yourself, Nancy," Mr. Holman said. "I'm afraid Miss Shannon is right. The GPS recorders for your team stopped a couple of hours ago."

"Nancy Drew would never cheat," Mrs. Mahoney said, joining us. "I'm sure she has a perfect explanation for everything. Don't you, Nancy?"

"Actually I do," I said. "Mrs. Mahoney, Mr. Holman, could I please talk with you in private? And would you ask Chief McGinnis to join us?"

"Certainly, Nancy," Mrs. Mahoney answered. "Let's go in the bank, shall we?"

"Nancy!" Bess yelled. "Where have you been?" Bess asked, rushing up. George and Ned followed close behind her.

"I'm okay, but what about you three?" I asked. "Mr. Holman says we were wiped off the GPS screen."

"Why don't you ask Deirdre?" George said. "I'm sure she can clear it up—right, DeeDee?"

"The only thing to get clear is that I won this race, Georgia," Deirdre snarled. She had been joined by one of the Jensens—they looked so much alike, I couldn't tell which one.

Ned pulled me away from Deirdre. "We had all

144

sorts of problems," he told me. "Bess wrecked your bike on a treacherous part of the course that was mysteriously covered with slippery gravel. My bike lost half its cogset, and George's had some weird steering problem that even Bess couldn't repair. We're sure Deirdre's team was behind all of it—but of course, we have no proof. I mean, other than the fact that they were the only other team camped near us. We just drove in to file a report with the judges."

"I'm going to try something," I told him. I reached into one of the panniers without opening it all the way. Then I pulled out the brass Gemini medallion and wandered casually back to where Bess, George, Deirdre, and Whoever Jensen stood.

"Now what?" Deirdre said. "If you think you're going to talk the race judges into taking away our rightful win, you're way wrong," she told me.

"Actually, I had a question for your teammate here." I showed the brass medallion to the twin. "Is this yours by any chance? You mentioned you were a Gemini, and—"

His hand shot toward my palm as he interrupted me. "Where did you find that?" he asked. "I've been looking all over for it." Okay, obviously he recognized the medallion.

"Curiously enough, I found it under Ned's car seat," I said, smiling at him.

"Then there's no way it could be yours, Thad," Deirdre cut in, glaring at her teammate. "Isn't that right?"

Thad looked a little surprised, but he pulled his hand back quickly and mumbled a low "Yes, I guess you're right."

"I don't know what you're up to," Deirdre said to me, her green eyes narrowed to squinty slits. "But it's not going to work. Come on, Thad."

She turned and the two of them marched off in a lockstep of black and blue.

"What about the money?" Bess asked. "Did you find it?"

"It's cool," I said with a grin, patting the panniers.

"You got it?" Ned shouted. "Unbelievable!"

"Shhhh," I warned my friends. "Most people don't even know that it was gone—let alone that it's back."

I couldn't take my eyes off Deirdre and Thad. She had pulled him over to the bench near the birdbath in the park across from the bank. It was the same bench where I had talked to Luther the day before. Deirdre looked like she was in her take-no-prisoners mode and giving Thad a real earful. In the background I could hear an announcer saying that if everyone would just be patient, the winning team would be introduced momentarily.

I handed Ned the panniers. "You three go on into

the bank," I told my team. "Tell Mrs. Mahoney and the others that I'll be right there."

Ned, Bess, and George followed Chief McGinnis, Mr. Holman, and Mrs. Mahoney into the bank. I walked around the crowd and ducked behind a large shrub in the small park. I was just a few yards from where Deirdre sat with her back to me. I could barely see her through the shrubbery, but I could hear every word.

"I can't believe you'd do something so stupid," she said. "Nancy was trying to set you up, and you almost fell for it!"

"Hey," Thad answered her. "That medallion is important to me. It was a gift from a special friend."

"I don't care," Deirdre snarled. "The plan from the very beginning was a few competitive pranks with the bikes during the race. Punctured tubes, oiled gravel, destabilized steering—all approved, all effective. I even said rattle them a little with Ned's bike the night before."

"And we did," Thad said with pride. "Right there on campus in open daylight. One of us stands guard, the other snips the chain."

"Keep your voice down," Deirdre hissed. "But I told you then and I'm telling you now—rolling that car into the creek was a mistake. That was going too far."

"We couldn't resist," Thad said, his voice lower.

"When we drove back to town, there was his car just sitting there. It was too easy. And we *didn't* roll the car into the creek. I just released the emergency brake. It rolled in on its own."

"Not funny," Deirdre said. "I'm warning you. Forget the stupid medallion and keep your mouth shut. And tell your brother and Malcolm to do the same."

Deirdre turned and headed back toward the finish line. She passed so close to the shrubbery that concealed me that I clamped my hand over my mouth and nose, so she wouldn't hear me breathe. I waited until Thad followed after her. Then I circled back around the crowd and into the bank.

Inside, Mrs. Mahoney, Chief McGinnis, Mr. Holman, and my team of friends waited for me.

I told them everything that had happened since lunch the previous day. Then I handed over the money.

The initial reaction was a celebration. Everyone congratulated me and asked a lot of questions.

"I'm shocked that Officer Rainey would do such a thing," Mrs. Mahoney said.

"He had access as the guard, and must have made the money-newspaper switch when no one was looking," I pointed out. "When he found out his car was out of commission, he got his bike back from his brother, and put the cash in a set of panniers. What better camouflage could there be for slipping out

148

of town on racing day than to be just another biker cycling down the street?"

Mrs. Mahoney and Mr. Holman were thrilled to get the money back of course. Mr. Holman pumped my arm in a powerful handshake. Mrs. Mahoney wrapped me in a hug scented with luxurious perfume.

Chief McGinnis held back, but gave me a grudging nod. I could tell I'd better smooth his feathers a little. I didn't want to lose him as an information source.

"Chief, you'll want to talk to Jasper Rainey," I said. "I don't think he was involved in the theft with his brother, but you're such an ace interrogator, I'm sure you can get the truth out of him."

Chief McGinnis nodded again and flashed me one of his rare smiles. "I've already done that, Nancy. He has an airtight alibi."

"My team sacrificed a lot in order to enable me to get the money back where it belonged," I reminded the officials. "They definitely deserve part of the credit."

"I think they deserve more than that," Mr. Holman said. "Technically you came across the line first, Nancy. I would be willing to declare your team to be the winner. I'm sure everyone would agree with me when they hear the full story."

"Everyone but Deirdre Shannon," George grumbled. "If you had any idea of—"

"George," I interrupted, "let's have a team conference."

I led George, Bess, and Ned over to a corner of the bank, while Mr. Holman and Mrs. Mahoney locked the money safely away. I could hear Chief McGinnis phoning his colleagues in the capital and advising them to pick up Officer Rainey. Through the window I could see the other four teams pedaling across the finish line.

"Nancy, we have to tell them what she did," Bess said. "It's not fair otherwise. I'm not saying we have to win, but Deirdre's team shouldn't either. Not after two days of dirty tricks and sabotage—even if we can't prove it."

I told my friends the exchange I'd overheard in the park between Deirdre and Thad.

"That's it," George said with a tone of disgust. "I understand that we can't rightfully be the winners. Nancy wasn't even in the race anymore. But maybe we could suggest that the team that came in *after* Deirdre's be declared the winner."

"Wait a minute," I said. "What's the whole point of the race?"

"To collect money for the Open Your Heart Fund," Bess answered.

"Exactly," I agreed. "Mr. Shannon pledged to add a thousand dollars to the total if his daughter won. So we can either let her take the Golden Anvil and ensure that there's a thousand more dollars available for the cause, or we can—"

"Okay, okay," George conceded. "You're right. It *is* called 'Open Your Heart' after all." She put out her arm, and we clasped hands and shot them up into the air one last time for this year's Biking for Bucks.

Then we told Mrs. Mahoney our decision.

"A *wonderful* solution," Mrs. Mahoney said. "Thank you so much!"

"I see Mr. Holman is out of jail," I said. "Is everything okay on that front?"

"Of course," Mrs. Mahoney said. "He won't be charged with anything. He's been completely cleared." She smiled warmly at me and my team.

"What would we have done without you, Nancy?" she said. "Because of you and your friends, everyone wins!"

"Except Officer Rainey," Ned said. "He loses, big-time."

"As well he should," Mrs. Mahoney said. "My only regret is that I won't see his face when he opens his panniers."

We all walked back out to the crowded celebration on Main Street.

"Oh, well," I said, "he'll have plenty of time to read all those newspapers. In prison!"

She's sharp.

She's smart.

She's confident.

She's unstoppable.

And she's on your trail.

MEET THE NEW NANCY DREW

Still sleuthing,

still solving crimes,

but she's got some new tricks up her sleeve!

NANCY DREW

girl detective